Safety Strip

"Let's have the robe," Shayne said.

Deedee pulled it together defensively. "I won't try to get away. I won't budge an inch."

Shayne continued to hold out his hand.

"But—" She shrugged out of the robe and gave it to him. "What if somebody comes in here for something?"

Shayne grinned. "Hold still. They'll think you're a statue."

GUILTY AS HELL

BRETT HALLIDAY

A DELL BOOK

Dell ® TM 681510, Dell Publishing Co., Inc.

Manufactured in the United States of America
First Printing—November 1967

GUILTY AS HELL

CHAPTER 1

Hal Begley, president and sole owner of Hal Begley Associates, buzzed his secretary.

"Ask Miss Morse to come in, please."

He did a quick isometric exercise while he waited. A big, well-tailored man in his middle thirties, Begley had the look of a former college athlete. In his business, the façade was important. As a matter of cold fact, he had lasted a single semester at a second-rate college, and he was totally uninterested in athletics He was doing well. Two years earlier his taxable income had passed $100,000. His firm occupied a suite of offices in a high-rent building on North Miami Avenue, and Begley himself owned an oceanfront property in Coconut Grove. His manner was crisp, genial and self-assured, and it concealed the fact that he was beginning to lose his nerve.

Candida Morse, his executive assistant, came in from an adjoining office. She was younger than Begley, a blonde in a pink suit that had originated in the workrooms of a famous New York designer. She wore it well. She was a slender girl with delicately carved features. She looked smart and ambitious, and in her case it was more than a façade. She was very smart and very ambitious, as her employer had reason to know.

Begley also knew he was lucky to have her. When she first came to work for him, he had been operating out of a two-desk office in a less desirable building in a scruffier section of Miami. He had owed money all over town. At that time he had called himself a "management consultant." His main job had been investigating applicants for executive openings. Candida shifted the firm immediately into recruitment and went on from there. Begley had the greatest respect for his assistant, but sometimes he was also a little scared of her.

"Isn't that a new jacket?" she said pleasantly. "Nice."

"For the Georgia weekend," he said, "to shore up the old morale. Did you get the guest list?"

She dropped a paper on his desk, which was a thick slab of walnut with the knotholes left in, and came around beside him so they could read it together. Begley had various pressing things on his mind, but his hand automatically slid up her leg beneath the pink skirt.

"From my good friend Walter Langhorne," Candida said. "There may be some last-minute additions, but as of last night, this is it. I'm meeting him for lunch. He'll pass on any developments."

"Candida baby, how would we ever get anything done around here without you?"

His hand stopped as it reached the coarse weave of her stocking top. His eye had skipped down the list to pick up the final name. For an instant he felt trapped, as though his tall leather chair had snapped shut on him.

"Michael Shayne? They didn't tell me Shayne was going to be there."

Candida bent down, took his face between her competent hands and kissed him. After a moment he felt himself beginning to relax. His hand slid on up to the cool flesh of her thigh. Completing the kiss, she looked at his face critically and wiped lipstick from his mouth.

"This explains a few things. A quiet duck-shooting weekend away from the telephone, to talk to a group of Despard executives about their high-level personnel problems? I never believed it for a minute, Hal, and neither did you. They want to talk to you quietly, all right—about how the T-239 report got out of the E. J. Despard safe into the hands of United States Chemical. And we don't know a thing about that, do we, darling?"

"You're talking a foreign language," Begley said, with the beginnings of a grin. "I'm a poor misunderstood head-hunter, and I wouldn't know an industrial secret if it came up and bit me on the ankle. Scout's honor. That's my story and I'm sticking to it even if they put lighted matches under my fingernails. If it was just a bunch of third-class vice-presidents, I wouldn't worry. The only thing is, Mike Shayne."

Candida went to the other side of the desk and dropped into a sling chair. She lit a cigarette which she took from a box on Begley's desk, using a tall desk lighter.

"Hal, having Shayne there only makes it official. We've known you were in for a grilling. I think the tactic we decided to follow is still perfectly sound. United States Chemical is moving up the announcement of the new paint to next Tuesday morning. I'm sorry the Despard people found out, but we expected it, after all. How can they hurt us, Hal, seriously?"

"You did a great job on it, baby. Great all the way. But there's four days between now and Tuesday. We can be hurt, believe me."

"I really don't see how." She frowned at the toe of her shoe, which was swinging in a short arc. "I'm not trying to be superoptimistic. If we get past the Tuesday announcement without publicity, United States owes us an extra thirty thousand. Conceivably we might lose that. But in the long run there's no such thing as bad publicity for us. There may be some tut-tutting. We may draw a couple of disapproving editorials. But the next time some company needs a piece of trade information and can't get hold of it through regular channels, they'll think of us."

"Not if Despard gets out an injunction."

"Hal, be reasonable. United States changed the formula enough so there can't be an action for infringement. Two companies were simply working on parallel lines. They both came up with a new kind of house paint that won't peel or blister, and United States, which is faster-moving, more aggressive and less conservative, got its product on the market first. It's that simple. Everybody in the paint business will know where they got their information. Proving it in court is another matter entirely."

"I hope you're right," Begley said. "But what if some clever bastard like Shayne gets our man to sign a confession?"

She smiled and shook her head. "We're covered there."

He knocked on the walnut desktop to take the curse off her flat statement. She could spot him fifty points on a comparative IQ, but he'd been around the business long enough to know that sometimes people didn't behave logically or predictably, especially if they happened to be a little eccentric to start with.

She went on, "Mike Shayne—now there's a paper tiger if I ever saw one. We didn't come off too badly the last time we tangled with him."

"I'm glad you think so, baby," Begley said sourly. "We came out with our skin. Barely. Three people retired early, one company paid a ten-thousand-buck fine, and Shayne knocked down a large fee."

"And the word-of-mouth got us the United States account. And dear God, was he lucky. That sort of a run can't go on forever. Stop thinking about last time, Hal. You can handle this man with one thumb and one forefinger. I want to brief you on the rest of the guests. Forbes Hallam, the president. He probably won't impress you, but bear in mind that E. J. Despard was doing an annual business of less than half a million dollars when he took over, and you know where they are now. Forbes Hallam, Jr.—he has a literary act. Commerce is beneath him and Henry James is his favorite writer. You might try to remember that. Walter Langhorne—the point to bear in mind there is that he and Mr. Hallam have come up together through the company, but they're very different types. There are all sorts of undercurrents. Jose Despard—Hallam's wife was his sister. Head of Research and Development, apparently not much between the ears. It's his family's old firm and he has a sizeable stock position. Richardson and Hall are two more vice-presidents. Richardson—"

Begley, on the other side of the desk, tried to concentrate on what she was saying as she continued down the list. It was hard to do because of his rising panic.

Coming out of his office, Jose Despard found his secretary, Miss Mainwaring, bending over a file drawer. Viewed from the front, Miss Mainwaring was tight-lipped and flat-chested, the everlasting spinster. But from this angle, her personality seemed to offer certain possibilities. What if Despard should favor her with a small, innocent tweak, purely as a sporting proposition? She would be startled at first. She would straighten so abruptly that she would give her pelvis a painful knock against the file. But after that, who could tell? Perhaps she would turn slowly, remove her glasses and remark in that sultry tone that had aroused Mrs. Despard's suspicions the first time she heard it on the phone, "I never knew you thought of me in that light, Mr. Despard."

He thrust both hands deep in his pockets to keep them out of harm's way. "Going to lunch. Don't forget to call the gun shop. Tell them I'll pick up the gun before five."

Straightening, Miss Mainwaring turned her spinsterish side in his direction. It became safe to take his hands out of his pockets. Imagine pinching the rear of anybody with a face like that!

"And if Mrs. Despard calls," he added, "tell her I'll be going straight to the airport from here. I'll phone her the minute we get in."

He went out, hatless. He was tall, very thin, and always seemed to be in a hurry, having important business to transact when he got where he was going. He wore his hair long over his ears. It was touched with gray; he was fifty-three. He sometimes managed to forget his age for as long as three or four days at a time.

He picked up a red Thunderbird convertible in the executive parking lot. Walter Langhorne, head of the design department, was backing a new Chrysler out of the next slot. The two men waved and left the lot by opposite exits. Another early lunch for Walt, Despard noted, and the lucky son of a bitch could stay out as long as he liked, with no fear that some clacking idiot would see him and pass the news along to his wife. Because he had no wife. Despard cocked an eyebrow, a wry expression which he had practiced so long it had become habitual. He believed it made him look English.

E. J. Despard, a family-operated chemical company with an antiquated plant in a small town in southern Georgia, had moved into plastics and synthetic fibers after the second world war and now had manufacturing facilities all over the country as well as in Europe. Largely through Jose Despard's efforts, the head office, as well as Research and Development, his own baby, had been transferred from Georgia to a new industrial park on undeveloped land between Miami and North Miami. The climate was better, the ocean was nearby, and there was a certain amount of extracurricular action if you knew how to go about locating it.

Despard drove east to the Expressway, picking it up at 103rd Street, and zoomed south toward Miami at a rate of speed that fitted the way he was feeling. He left the Expressway at the 54th Street exit. A block or so later, he stopped at an outside phone booth. Returning to his car, he pressed a button which brought the top up out of the boot. He seldom used the Thunderbird's top, and it felt like a disguise.

He cruised north into Edison Center.

He felt absently for a stick of gum and chewed it down to manageable size. This was another effort at camouflage. The head of one of the oldest and finest families in Georgia naturally was seldom seen with gum in his mouth.

He turned left at Edison Park, and his heart gave a thump. A girl got up off a bench and slanted across the street toward him. He pulled up and waited. She gave a quick look around, yanked open the door and bolted inside.

She wasn't quite young enough to be his granddaughter. She was wearing a black turtleneck, a short skirt and sandals. She, too, was chewing gum, as rapidly and nervously as Despard himself. She had long black hair which never satisfied her, and every time she changed to a new hair style, she changed her personality to go with it. Today, partly because he had given her so little warning, it hung down lankly to her thin shoulders. She had a pointed face, bright restless eyes, too much lipstick. He had never seen her eat anything except French fries and hamburgers, and she was much too skinny. But in the black turtleneck her small breasts, he thought, were charming. At times she looked apathetic, but at other times she had all the energy of a broken high-tension wire.

"Honey," she complained as he drove off, "you said you wouldn't do that. What if Dad was home sick and picked up the phone?"

"Simple. I'd ask if this was Schwartz's delicatessen."

She sighed and settled deeper into the upholstery. "God, do I like these bucket seats."

"That's why I got them."

"Know what I'd like to do some day? Ride up Collins Avenue with the top down in a bikini."

"All right, you shall."

"Yeah, I bet! I saw it once, a blonde in a suit about the size of a postage stamp, and if you just sort of glanced, you'd think she was naked. In a Bird with red-leather buckets. The man, though! Jesus. A real creep with a cigar. Where are we supposed to be going?"

He leered, twirling imaginary mustaches. "Don't you know?"

"Jose, do you think we ought to?" she wailed. "In the daytime? Remember last week, you didn't get back to the office and you missed some dumb conference. I don't mind about me. I'll just tell Dad I went to a double feature, and who cares, anyway? I kind of had Sunday saved."

Despard signaled for a right turn. "Sunday's out, that's the trouble."

"Hell! Why?"

"I have to go on that damn company weekend," he said with disgust. "Shooting ducks—I haven't shot a duck for twenty years. Any time I want to eat duck, I'll go to a restaurant and order a tame one. But the word has come down from Mt. Olympus—be there. Apparently we're after something bigger than duck, wearing pants."

"Come on, Jose. Pants?"

"It's too complicated to explain. And to make it look good, I have to get up before dawn and stand out in the mud. I know that marsh. I know it well. The mosquitoes are twice as big as the ducks."

"I don't get it! What's the good of being the brother-in-law of the head of a company if you can't make any plans? You already gave him forty hours this week."

"I know, sweetie, it's rough. But this is top priority and I can't do a thing about it."

"You don't have to give me a big story. You wouldn't have another girl on the string, would you?"

He smiled. "Funny face."

"I had a chance to go somewhere else Sunday, that's all," she said discontentedly. "I said I was going to be busy."

He took a small package out of his side pocket and passed it to her.

"A present?" she cried, with one of her fast personality switches.

She was now a little girl on Christmas morning. She broke the string and unwrapped a small perfume box. Despard was attending to the traffic, but he could tell she was disappointed. Then she opened the box and read the label, and her jaws stopped moving.

"Jose, this stuff sells for fifty bucks an ounce, and this is an ounce!"

He twirled his imaginary mustache again. "I expect to get my money's worth."

"Don't worry about that. I never heard you complain yet." She put a hand on his nearest leg. "I don't like that about Sunday, but I'll just have to stand it. I'll ask my girl friend to come over and give me a permanent. But I'll have to pour this perfume in another bottle or change the label, one. If she sees it, she's going to want to know what's going on. The way she pokes and pries and picks, I just know I'll tell her the whole thing."

"Wouldn't she approve?"

"Oh, I don't know. She might be a little jealous."

She giggled suddenly.

"What?" he said, smiling.

She shot him a glance. "I just had a way-out idea, I don't know what you'd think. She's mad! My girl friend, absotively, posolutely mad. And if I give her a small sniff of this perfume, she'll purr like a cat. The next time we have a date, why don't we ask her along?"

His face sobered. So did hers.

"Honey? It was just a thought that happened to cross my mind."

Despard moistened his lips. He could feel his heart hammering unpleasantly.

"What's she like?"

She settled into the embrace of the comfortable bucket seat. "Cute as a button. Everybody says so. Much cuter than me. But goodness, it's entirely up to you." She made a small movement. "Honey, I wouldn't want you to get picked up for speeding, but could you please hurry?"

In the main parking lot in Crandon Park on Key Biscayne, Walter Langhorne waited in his Chrysler. He had parked carelessly, the front wheels blocking access to the next parking space. Seeing a red Volkswagen coming off the Bear Cut Bridge, he started his motor, maneuvered forward and back, and opened up the space.

Candida Morse turned in and parked. She was wearing her elegant pink suit. As she swung out of her low-slung car, her skirt rode up to give Langhorne a fast glimpse of the loveliest legs in Greater Miami.

Langhorne had an air which his colleague, Jose Despard, failed to achieve through trying too hard—he looked as though he lived on a private income. He was well aware that to begin with, Candida had sought him out solely because he was a chemical-company vice-president with an itchy foot, and she was a wheel in a well-known headhunting firm. They had both put themselves out to be agreeable. This had been easy to sustain. Each had quickly discovered the other to be handsome, civilized, intelligent, a little cynical, very good company. They had met a dozen times, either behind closed doors or in unlikely places, as they were meeting now. Once they stole an afternoon and drove to a secluded beach on one of the Lower Keys. Each time, as they parted, Langhorne wished they had met in a different way. He had begun to wonder in the last few days if, by being a bit more difficult, he could have maneuvered her to his apartment and into his bed. Probably not, he thought. He was uncommitted and would remain so.

He brought a long-necked bottle of German wine over from the cooler in the back seat and was working the corkscrew when she opened the door and got in beside him.

"Rhine wine," she observed. She uncovered two earthenware bowls in a wicker basket. "Vichysoisse. Watercress and cucumber sandwiches. Walter, why haven't you ever been snapped up by somebody?"

"I've been too fast on my feet," he replied, drawing the cork. "How do you know some charmer didn't turn me down once and I've never been able to forget her?"

"I'd accept that," Candida said, laughing. "Is it true?"

"I forget."

He was busy for a moment arranging napkins and silverware. He took the chilled glasses out of the cooler and poured the wine. They touched glasses.

Langhorne said seriously, "To your success, if that's truly what you want."

"It's what I want. But why so ceremonious? You sound as though the next thing you say will be goodbye."

He nodded. "It's our last meeting. In the present series. I'll call you in six months' time and see what you think about starting over on a different basis."

"Then you've decided not to go with United States Chemical?"

"Almost."

She disposed of the matter with a little movement of her lips. "That's out of the way."

"Candida, one more moment on business. We've always been able to understand each other, I think, without elaborate explanations. I don't want to change the rules, but I do want to say this. I'm not one of the most loyal employees E. J. Despard ever had, and if you find yourself in any difficulty and there's anything I can do to help, will you let me know?"

She put her hand against his face. "You really are a

lovely man, Walter. But this is one time I don't think I do understand you."

"Something's going on," he said slowly. "I've probably given you a biased picture of our distinguished president. Hallam has never had any real existence for me outside of his role in the firm, but I learned long ago never to underestimate him. I told him I was considering an offer from one of our competitors—"

She broke in. "When?"

"Yesterday. If I hadn't known him so well, I would have thought he showed emotion. We've been at exactly opposite poles on every decision, every attitude, every course of action. I would have said he'd be delighted to be shut of me. But on the contrary. I haven't definitely said I'd stay, but if I do I'll have ten thousand dollars more a year, complete autonomy, a big increase in the design budget, veto power over a broad range of policy, six months out of every eighteen in Europe—"

"Walter, that's marvelous!"

"I agree. But unless I've been dead wrong about Forbes Hallam all these years, something's behind it. He wants me on the scene, but why?"

He moved his wine glass so it caught the light. "And I'm wondering, in a perverse way, if he's been told that I've been seeing you."

"Would that be so ghastly?"

"Darling, of course not. Unless by some odd chance he connects it with the flap we've been having about a certain new nonpeelable paint known to our advertising department as T-239."

Neither spoke for a moment. Langhorne tasted his cold soup and added a few grains of pepper from a pepper mill.

Candida ventured, "How does that concern me?"

Langhorne chose his words carefully. "We're all of us sitting on a barrel of dynamite. I wouldn't be surprised to see the roof blow off the administration building before the end of the week. There's a directors' meeting on Thursday, and the board is split down the middle. Hallam's enemies have been waiting for a pretext to move. I think you ought to pass this on to Begley. I'm not too impressed with your employer, as a matter of fact. It may be a mistake for him to go to Georgia this weekend. I want you to consider seriously having him come down with a virus that will keep him in bed until after the board meeting."

"He's not exactly a fool, Walter."

"Would you mind defining your terms?" Langhorne said dryly. "It's not his brain I'm thinking about. It's whether he can be trusted. We have a report that you've been seen going into the United States Chemical offices on Route 128 outside of Boston. Not Hal Begley, you see. Candida Morse. I'm usually right about these things. He has a bad eye. What that eye tells me is that Hal Begley in the clutch will think of Hal Begley, and of nobody else. If he has to jettison someone in order to survive, too bad for that someone. Hal Begley Associates will dwindle down to Hal Begley Period."

He spooned up some soup. "I hate the idea of the kind of throat-cutting and back-stabbing I'm in for this weekend. Blood will flow! It's no concern of mine who wins, the Hallams or the Despards. Probably I should have turned Hallam down outright instead of asking for a few days to think about it. One reason I didn't was that I'd like to be on the inside when the trouble starts. Perhaps I can help. I've become very fond of you, my dear."

He touched her knee. "Come, Candida, you're not eating."

Forbes Hallam, Jr., a good-looking, dark-haired young man with the build of a quarter-miler, tapped on a door on the twelfth floor of the Hotel St. Albans in Miami Beach. Without waiting for an answer, he unlocked it with a key he carried on his key ring and went in.

It was 5:15 in the afternoon, and the blinds were drawn. The room was awash with discarded clothing. An empty gin bottle lay on the carpet. Ruth Di Palma was asleep on the bed amid a tumble of bedclothes. She was face down, one bare arm trailing.

Forbes adjusted the blind cords, letting in the afternoon

sun. This room was on the Inland Waterway side of the hotel, where prices were lower. Ruth, in fact, occupied it rent-free during the off-season, although she was supposed to be ready to move on an hour's notice.

He switched on the exhaust fan and turned the air-conditioning dial up a notch. Sitting on the bed beside the sleeping girl, he slipped his hand under the covers.

"Ruthie, wake up."

He moved his hand along her body. She stirred, murmuring, then flopped over, opened her eyes suddenly and stared up at him. It was clear to Forbes that she didn't have the remotest idea who he was. Her skin was a lovely golden color. Her face glistened with something she had rubbed on it before going to bed. The sun had burned her hair the color of driftwood. There were no lines on her face, and, if it was true that anxiety was what put the lines on people's faces, Forbes could be fairly sure that she would still look the same at sixty.

"You remember me," he said, withdrawing his hand.

"Put your hand back. Come on."

"Ruthie—"

She lifted the sheet. She slept without nightgown or pajamas.

"What are you doing out there with all those clothes on?"

"Ruth, it's five in the afternoon, which is a peculiar time to be asleep, and I tore in from the office to see you for about ten seconds."

"I took a pill. Or two. Or a handful. I love you."

"I love you."

"Five in the afternoon? You don't scare me a bit. The real point is, what day?"

Forbes laughed. "Friday."

"Well, if it's still only Friday." She pulled at his clothes. "Be unconventional. Come to bed. I haven't seen you since this morning."

He scuffed off his loafers. Without undressing any further, he swung in under the sheet and took her in his arms.

"Don't you want to know why I left the office early and

drove like a madman and why I'm taking a chance on holding up the company plane?"

"Why?"

"I wanted to find out what you decided."

"I never decide things," she said. "Things decide themselves."

He gave her a small shake. "Why don't you marry me, Ruthie?"

"Because you're only one person. If you have to have a reason."

He laughed again. "I'm changeable."

"Not enough. Number two, you like your job."

"I hate my job," he said calmly.

"You only think you hate it. Let's make love. I don't feel a bit like it. It's the last thing I'd suggest ordinarily, down at the end of the list after watching cartoons on TV. But anything to change the subject!"

"Ruthie, don't," he said, trying to keep her from unbuttoning his shirt. "I have to be at Opa-Locka airport in sixty minutes, or my father will chop me off at the neck. He likes people to be on time."

Doubling the pillow behind her, she hitched up against the headboard and looked at him balefully. "You won't believe this, but do you know I forgot you were going away? Now maybe you'll agree I'm not cut out to be the wife of a rising young executive. I told Freddy and Adrian we'd go to Palm Beach."

"Where in Palm Beach?"

"Freddy met the lady who gives those millions of dollars to the opera. She has some wonderful Picassos and he's going to get her to give him one."

"Nobody gives Freddy Picassos."

"He has a plan worked out. I'll see if he can put it off a week. Then I promised we'd be back in time for the soul session at the Stanwick. They've got some real weirdies."

"I'll be satisfied to miss that."

"Too bad for you, buster. I'll go stag. Cigarette."

She watched him find the cigarettes and hunt around in the mess for matches. "It begins to come back to me. I wish you wouldn't keep telling me things when I'm tight. This is your Mike Shayne weekend."

"There, you see? There's nothing wrong with your memory."

He held a match to her cigarette. She breathed out smoke and looked at him.

"Forbes, are you in any kind of jam I don't know about?"

He shook his long hair off his forehead. "I tell you about all my jams."

"At three or four in the morning, when I couldn't care less. I asked a couple of people about this Mike Shayne, and here's what they tell me. Now listen. To start with, you have to remember he's tricky. But he's not like other tricky people. He can be tough. And he's not like most tough people because he can also be tricky. If you can't follow that, it's because I'm not at my best before breakfast. What it boils down to, if you've got something you don't want Shayne to find out, don't take your eyes off the radar screen."

"Shayne and I are working the same side of the street. We're the one-two punch for the good guys."

"Hmm."

"Ruthie, are you worrying about me by any chance?"

"Me worry? About you? You may not be handsome, but you're rich, accomplished, a talented writer, with a nice car, nice clothes and a nice crusty father." She added, "You did raise that money O.K., didn't you?"

"Ruthie, that was ages ago. It all blew over. You realize, don't you, that if you've started to worry about me and money, you might as well marry me? Wives are supposed to worry about their husbands. Girls are supposed to be blasé about their boy friends."

"How can I marry you, Forbes? I'm five years older than you."

"I'll catch up."

"Besides, your father's paying me a weekly allowance as long as we don't get married."

His smile vanished. He seized her bare arm above the elbow. "Is that true?"

She looked at him in silence for a moment before shaking her head. "No."

He let go. "Well, your financial condition's a mystery to me, but I really don't think that explains it. The old man's attached to that dough. He made it himself. I've got to go."

"Not yet."

"Yes, damn it, if I want to hang onto that job, and we've been through that ten million times. If I could get along without eating, I could easily live on what I make writing fiction. Three short stories in six months, two hundred and twenty-five dollars."

"You're not using the old computer," she said, tapping his forehead. "If you drive to Opa-Locka, you'll just about make it, leaving now. The Watson Park heliport is five minutes from here. Take a helicopter.

He looked into her eyes, then glanced quickly at his watch.

"You see?" she said. "Call the heliport."

She threw off the sheet and slid down in the bed, watching him gravely. He hooted and reached for the phone, beginning to unbutton his shirt with the other hand.

CHAPTER 2

In a crudely-built duck blind in a Georgia salt marsh early the next morning, Forbes Hallam, Jr., held out a cup of steaming coffee to the big redheaded private detective named Michael Shayne.

Shayne leaned against the stringer at the front of the blind, a 12-gauge semiautomatic resting lightly in the crook of one arm. His slouch was characteristic, and characteristically deceptive. He had an athlete's ability to seem totally relaxed a second before erupting into a violent explosion of controlled energy. A bloody mallard, brought down by Shayne in his first shot of the morning, lay on a bench at the back of the blind.

"Coffee?" Forbes said.

The detective took the cup, set it on the stringer and added cognac from a pint bottle. He offered the bottle to young Hallam, who was sitting on the bench well back from the opening, his long legs stretched out in front of him. His shotgun was propped in a corner. He had yet to take a shot.

"Change your mind and have some cognac?" Shayne said.

The young man shook his head ruefully. "I'd better wait. I had too much Scotch last night, I'm ashamed to say."

"You're not the only one."

Forbes laughed. "Begley! I've never seen anybody get stoned faster."

Shayne straightened. Crinkles of concentration appeared at the corners of his eyes. A flight of blacks had appeared in the southeast, three ranges high. Pulling out a slender duck call, Shayne began working them down. He started with a piercing highball, followed by a series of high excited notes. The flight wheeled. The Chesapeake retriever beside his knee watched alertly. Shayne talked the ducks down and down. They were at sixty yards, coming over the blocks on the cross wind, when they were spooked by a single shot from another blind. They veered up and away. Shayne swore.

"My uncle Jose," Forbes said. "He always was a lousy judge of distance."

After lighting a cigarette, Shayne said, "Your father told me you'd fill me in. This might be a good time."

"I suppose," Forbes said with a sigh. "I knew he had that in mind when he put us together. I just wish the aspirin would take hold, that's all. How much has he told you?"

"Enough so I can start with a couple of questions. What's this T-239 paint?"

"The name doesn't mean a thing, Mr. Shayne. The 'T' stands for the pigment—titanium dioxide. Adding the number is just a gimmick, to make it sound scientific for the ads and the label. It's an alkyd resin, water-thinned, and there's no question it's a damn good paint. We're planning to offer an absolute three-year money-back guarantee against peeling or blistering on bare wood using a recommended primer. I don't know how much you know about house paint—"

"I live in a hotel."

"You're lucky—I think I'll have some of the cognac after all. This coffee isn't doing anything for me."

The detective splashed a dollop of cognac in the younger man's coffee cup.

Forbes went on: "I don't know how people who own houses manage to keep their sanity. Father maintains that the reason outside paints break down so fast is that houses are better insulated and present-day appliances give off so much steam—dishwashers, humidifiers, driers. The steam has to go somewhere. It breaks the paint seal and exits by way of a blister, which then peels down to the wood. The public, of course, simply figures we're marketing an inferior product, to break down faster so we can sell more paint. This worries my father. Where will it end? In government regulation, he thinks. Socialism."

He snorted scornfully and sipped at his coffee. "Hey, this is good. Maybe we ought to add a few drops of cognac to each gallon of paint and see if it lasts any longer." He winced. "I'm not really up to being facetious this early in the morning. God knows, it's serious. We must have a couple of million dollars invested in T-239. The first company out with a really nonpeelable product is going to mop up. Everybody's been working on it. Well, about eighteen months ago we came up with a formula that gave very good lab results. That didn't necessarily mean it would stand up well on a house. We put it through an elaborate series of tests, and those tests can't be hurried. There's really no substitute for slapping a coat of paint on a piece of cedar siding and leaving it out in different kinds of weather. Sure enough, after a few months the white paint turned yellow. We took care of that and all the technical boys are very pleased with the way things have turned out. But Dad happens to believe in being two hundred percent certain. That's how we've got caught. He ordered a new series of tests, and we can't hope to have T-239 in the stores before next May at the earliest."

"And United States Chemical stole the formula?"

"More than the formula. The really important thing was the test results. A year and a half is a long time to keep a secret in any business. By not having to duplicate the tests, they save a huge amount of money and cut months off the development period. We've been getting rumbles about a new indestructible paint they're about to launch with a long-term guarantee. They did a fair job of keeping it under wraps, but we finally managed to purloin a can. And it's T-239, all right, with a few modifications. And a source in their experimental division tells us they rushed into production after a crash testing program that couldn't possibly prove anything about durability. They're making the first announcement on the CBS breakfast show next Tuesday morning. In other words, they'll beat us out by five months."

Without looking directly at him, Shayne had been studying the young man as he talked. He was twenty-five, Shayne judged. One moment he was caught up in his explanation, taking it with utter seriousness. A moment later he would make a clumsy gesture and seem to sneer at the importance of what he was saying. At times he was capable of producing a sudden, engaging grin. Having talked at length with the senior Hallam, Shayne knew the younger man's position in the company must be far from easy.

Shayne's gun came up.

"Ducks," he said in a low voice.

Forbes reached for his shotgun, then sat back with a flap of his hand. There were five pintails and a single, quartering in and rising. At first Shayne thought they were all his. As he tracked them, they veered more and more to the right, crossing at the extreme limits of his gun's range. There were two quick bangs from the next blind, a thousand feet distant. Two ducks plummeted out of the sky.

"Dad's still got his eye," Forbes remarked. "I assume

that was Dad and not Walter. Walter Langhorne and a shotgun are two different animals."

"You aren't shooting this morning?" Shayne said.

Forbes said defensively, "I'm too shaky. When I was a boy I used to come out here with Dad all the time. I don't see much point in it any more."

He sipped his coffee. "I'm beginning to feel hungry. Nothing like fresh air and not enough sleep. Let me finish, and maybe by then we won't get any dirty looks if we go back and have a decent breakfast. I was about to tell you about United States Chemical. They're teetering on the edge. They have a nice tax-loss position and Dad sees no reason why they shouldn't merge with E. J. Despard, through an exchange of stock, to everybody's benefit. They won't even discuss it. It's a Boston company, wholly owned by the Perkins family. We're Goliath and they're David, and in real life how often does David win? But this paint coup gives them a reprieve. By the time we stumble out with T-239, they'll have another ten percent of the market and much prestige, and maybe they can stay out of our clutches. What I'm really saying is, to put this in proportion, it's more important to them than it is to us. Dad never likes to come in second, but in the long run we probably won't even lose much money. But for United States it's life or death. Literally."

"What happens if you find out anything before Tuesday?"

"Well, we're coming down to the wire, Mr. Shayne. We'd need something so good we could go into court with it on Monday. Calling you in was Dad's idea. This weekend was mine, a kind of last-ditch expedient. I thought if we could get you and Begley here, plus enough of the rest of us to feed you leads and suggestions, something might give. Begley was foolish to accept, in my opinion. He probably thought it would be suspicious not to. You can question various people individually during the day and get your ammunition ready. Tonight we'll run an all-night poker game and put on the pressure. I don't know if you've heard about the soul sessions people have been having lately."

"The what?"

"They're called soul sessions. That's not a very good name for them. A bunch of people get together for a weekend. By that I mean sixty hours straight without sleep, in the same couple of rooms. For the first ten or twelve it's like any ordinary cocktail party. Everybody talks on the surface. Then in the middle of the next day you stop trying to impress people, because you're too tired. You get down to what's really on your mind. I've sat through a couple and they didn't do much for me, but I have friends who claim the experience changed their life. I don't mean we'll do any of that deep probing here."

Shayne said skeptically, "Your father agreed?"

Forbes gave a half laugh. "I didn't describe it quite like that to him. But he's been involved in around-the-clock bargaining sessions with union people, and he knows that funny things happen between two o'clock in the morning and daybreak. You forget the stereotypes, the prepared positions. You realize that the other people in the room are human beings."

"In Hal Begley's case I wouldn't go that far." Shayne poured more coffee from the big thermos. "Are you certain the Begley firm handled the theft?"

"Positive. Begley himself isn't directly involved. All the contacts have been handled by a girl named—"

He snapped his fingers. Shayne put in, "Candida Morse."

"Yes. Begley went on the United States payroll as a management consultant for three months at forty thousand a month. Needless to say, that hundred and twenty thousand didn't buy any management consulting, because he couldn't consult his way out of a paper bag. It bought a Xerox copy of a three-hundred-page report. Our source at United States copied one of those pages. The heading had been clipped off but otherwise it was word for word page ninety-nine of our T-239 material, which Walter Langhorne and I put together last spring."

Shayne thought for a moment. "How many copies did you make?"

"None at all. What we were doing was pulling the story together for the board of directors, so they could decide whether to budget for it at the June meeting. As a rule I get a little impatient with office security. Good Lord—we decide on a new advertising approach for some product, and the way we carry on you'd think it was plans and specs for a round-the-world missile. But the cloak and dagger stuff was justified on this one, even I could see that. It stayed in the safe and was only brought out for board members. They had to read it in the office under the eye of a certain Miss Phoebe McGonigle, who is so security-minded that she wouldn't let her own mother go to the bathroom without proper clearance. So we aren't talking about the kind of security lapse where some production worker sneaks into the super's office after the rest of the day shift has gone home. This came from somebody close to the top."

"How many possibilities, do you figure?"

"Maybe twenty, and some of those are pretty marginal. You'll want to look at the physical layout. There's no copying machine in that part of the building, for one thing. That washes out two or three possible suspects. Another was on the Coast when the transfer probably took place. And so on. I'd say it just about comes down to the people who are here this weekend."

"So it's not only Begley you're hoping to break."

"That's right. Even if we can't keep the United States paint off the market, we'd like to find out how it happened so it won't happen again. A strong minority on the board is opposed to the present management, by which I mean my father. T-239 is Dad's creation, but if he hadn't been so damn slow and conservative, if he hadn't insisted on that last test series, we'd be out with it now. So that's a point against him. On the other hand, if my Uncle Jose or anybody in the opposition group had anything to do with the leak, hoping to use it to discredit him, Dad can wipe up the floor with them. If he can prove it! I wish it was simpler, but that's why we're paying you ten thousand dollars, I guess."

"What's the explanation of the time lag? Why didn't you bring me in a couple of months ago? This isn't a job you can do on a weekend."

"We wanted to handle it inside the firm, if possible. This wasn't just my idea; everybody agreed. If there had to be publicity, we wanted to be able to control it."

"So right from the start," Shayne pointed out, "you expected to find you'd been sold out by one of your top men."

Forbes nodded. "Not necessarily for money. You know more about Begley than I do, but I understand he's been known to use blackmail."

"Sure. It's risky as hell, but cheaper in the short run."

"So the police had to be ruled out from the start. This is just not a police matter. And how many private investigators are smart enough to find out anything, and how many of those can you trust? Don't be offended," he said with his sudden grin.

Shayne returned the grin, beginning to like him a little better. "I see your problem. If Begley's been blackmailing one of your people, you don't want some slob of a private eye to get hold of it."

"Well, you must admit, Mr. Shayne, your profession isn't known for its high ethical standards. But Dad was talking to somebody at Pittsburgh Plate Glass last week, and your name came up. Apparently there's no love lost between you and Begley."

"You can say that again."

"The Pittsburgh man said that was the first time Begley had ever been beaten. Dad thought we could count on you to give it a little extra effort."

Shayne shook his head shortly. "I didn't beat him. I collected a fee. The client was satisfied, but I wasn't. Begley's still in business."

"Now wait," Forbes said. "Hold on a minute. We don't want to tie our hands. The only practical outcome I can foresee is a deal, under which Begley agrees to provide us with the name of his contact in return for an agreement from us not to take any legal action. We don't want your personal feelings to stand in the way if that kind of deal is the best we can get. Begley as an individual isn't all that important."

"He is to me," Shayne said evenly. "He's in a funny

business. He can win and lose at the same time. He's been using that Pittsburgh Plate Glass affair for advertising. It showed that, when he goes after information, he gets it, and he doesn't care what methods he uses so long as they get results. Good advertising for him is bad advertising for me. I didn't understand I was being hired to handle a deal. Maybe you'd better look for somebody else."

"Time's too short!" Forbes exclaimed. "You can grind Begley up and eat him in a bun for all I care. But to us, that isn't the main thing. See what you think this weekend."

Shayne waited a moment. "Who's been handling the investigation?"

"I have. Forbes Hallam, Jr., junior executive. I thought it might be more interesting than what I was doing, which was one step above emptying the wastebaskets. I didn't know what I was getting into. I thought the culprit would turn out to be a technician or white-collar worker with a grudge against Dad. If Dad had ever gone to business school, he would have flunked his human relations, I'm afraid. One of his favorite sayings is that he doesn't care about being popular, he cares about the quarterly dividend. This is old-fashioned enough to have a certain charm, especially if you happen to be a stockholder, but there are people in the company who—well, who hate him. Unfortunately, I couldn't come up with anybody who hated him and also had access to the report. It's beginning to look as though *I* stole the damn thing. I mean it. I did the actual writing on it, under Walter Langhorne's supervision. I tried to put the technical stuff into English. After Walter edited it, I did the proofreading. There was even one day when I got fed up with Miss Phoebe McGonigle and I didn't turn in the proof sheets. As soon as you start asking questions, Mr. Shayne, you'll find out that I'm not the typical eager-to-please trainee. I'm a trainee as a last resort, and I kicked and screamed all the time they were fastening on my button-down shirt and pulling up my executive-length socks."

He grinned again, making one of his abrupt shifts. "But the junior-executive racket isn't as bad as I expected. I've always wanted to be a writer. Dad gave me a year after college and I wrote a bunch of short stories. I sold a few. If you make the mistake of looking mildly interested, I'll press copies on you. Maybe some day I'll write about what goes on in the Despard administration building. The public would be amazed!"

"How long have you worked there, Forbes?"

"Two years. In my own opinion, I'm underpaid. I'm also not very good about making out personal budgets and crap like that, so I frequently find myself short of funds. I didn't steal any formulas, however. Formulae. I know that for a fact, even if nobody else does, so I haven't wasted any time investigating myself."

He took a sip of coffee. "I've picked up a certain amount of gossip, which I hope I can use if I ever get around to writing that novel. I didn't go hunting for it; it just drifted in. One of the first things I learned was that Hal Begley Associates isn't listed in the Yellow Pages as a spy firm. Ostensibly they're a chi-chi employment agency, handling nobody earning less than twenty thousand a year. Probably they even do some legitimate business along those lines, I don't know."

"Why not?" Shayne said. "That's the easiest way to pick up industrial secrets—hire somebody who can carry them out in his head."

"I hadn't thought of it that way. What I'm getting around to, slowly, is that Walter Langhorne and the girl from the Begley firm were seen together at an art auction in Palm Beach."

Shayne considered. "Has Langhorne said anything about changing jobs?"

"Mr. Shayne," Forbes said anxiously, "I feel like a fink! He's not only talked about changing jobs, he said something about tying up with United States Chemical, damn it! Naturally he told me in confidence, so if you use this, would you mind disguising where you got it? He's a friend of mine. He's easily the brightest man in the place."

"And he's still working there, which might mean that Candida tried and didn't get him."

"It might, or it might mean that he's taking a post-dated check. He cares what his friends think, and he wouldn't want them to think he's a thief. But I can't believe it, Mr. Shayne. It's perfectly true that he doesn't think he owes his main loyalty to E. J. Despard and Co. But he's one of the few people I know with any moral standards at all. There are more important things in Walter's life than the quarterly dividends."

A shotgun went off in the blind to their right. Glancing up, Shayne saw a single mallard almost directly overhead, climbing. He would have had a shot a second earlier, but it was too late now.

"And at that point," Forbes said, "I decided I was no longer running this investigation. The last thing I could do is go up to Walter Langhorne and ask him to explain what he was doing in Palm Beach with the sinister Candida Morse."

There was a hoarse, urgent shout. Shayne and Forbes looked at each other for an instant. Then Shayne whirled and stepped up out of the blind.

The senior Hallam burst from the adjoining blind, his crest of gray hair blowing in the wind. He had his tan hunting cap in his hand. He crunched it violently, threw it down in the reeds and banged his thigh with his fist.

Shayne splashed toward him. Hearing the sound, Hallam turned and waited. He was a short, plump man whose usual position was straight up and down, to get the maximum mileage out of his limited stature. He had a tight mouth, sharp, unfriendly eyes. Everything about his bearing showed that he wasn't in the habit of losing, and if he did lose occasionally, he would do it without grace. Now he had suddenly changed roles. He was breathing as though he had climbed a long flight of stairs.

"There's been a terrible accident," he said in a strained voice as Shayne reached him.

He made a distracted gesture and pressed both clenched fists to his chest. Shayne stooped and looked into the blind.

Walter Langhorne lay on the muddy duckboards. A magnum charge of 4's had caught him in the left cheekbone and there was nothing left of that side of his head.

CHAPTER 3

An intelligent-looking Labrador retriever whimpered beside the body. One shotgun, a fine lightweight English weapon, hung from a nail at the back of the blind. Another, a full-choked 20-gauge, lay on the boards at Langhorne's feet. Shayne's quick scrutiny of the blind picked up one other object of interest—a silver pocket flask on the bench.

Forbes, at Shayne's shoulder, made a sound as though he had been hit. Shayne turned back to the father. Hallam had dropped his hands and seemed to cringe away. A drop of saliva glistened at the corner of his mouth.

"How did it happen?" Shayne asked quietly.

"I don't know." Hallam stared at the water at his feet. "I just don't know."

He drew a long shuddering breath. His eyes started slowly up the redhead's rangy body. When they met Shayne's eyes he gave his head a short shake, as though awakening from a hard sleep.

The detective took out his pint of brandy. "Take some of this. You have to talk about it sooner or later. You might as well get it over with."

Hallam went on shaking his head. His hand started up to take the bottle, but he dropped it again.

"No. If they smell it they'll think I'm drunk. I'm cold sober. I drink very sparingly, Shayne. Four ounces of whiskey before dinner, sometimes a weak Scotch afterward. I never touch alcohol before lunch."

"Then that's Langhorne's flask in there?"

Hallam blinked again and his back straightened. He was beginning to recover, though both fists were still clenched. His son was vomiting into the long reeds at the end of the blind.

"The flask," Hallam said. "A silver flask. Yes, it's Walter's, of course. It cost a hundred and twenty-five dollars at Tiffany's in New York. I happen to know. A hundred and twenty-five dollars!" He made a quick, convulsive motion. "Shayne, he just sat there drinking, making barbed remarks. I've known him since I was ten years old. Stop that!" he told his son sharply. "Or go farther away."

His tall brother-in-law, Jose Despard, emerged from the next blind in the line. After a moment he came toward them, an awkward figure in too-large waders. Hallam scooped up a double handful of salt water and dashed it over his face. After doing this twice more, he straightened, dripping. This time he came back to his full height.

"Despard," he called, "What's the reason for the kaffeeklatsch? You people make one holy hell of a decoy. Especially you, Shayne, with that red hair."

Hallam said steadily, in something approaching his usual tone, "I just shot Walter."

"What?"

"The damn fool popped up in front of my gun."

Despard looked blank. He swiveled from Hallam toward Shayne. The detective told him, "We'll need the sheriff. Go in and phone."

Despard looked back at Hallam. "You shot Walter?" he said stupidly. *"Walter?"* Suddenly his eyes sharpened. "What makes you think he's the one? Have you gone out of your mind?"

"It was an accident," Hallam said coldly. "Let's everybody get that straight. Call the sheriff."

After a moment, Despard turned and headed for the jeep. Shayne offered Hallam a cigarette. Again the older man shook his head. Forbes, at the end of the blind, came erect. He was pale and shaken.

"The sheriff knows me," Hallam said. "His name's Banghart. What's his first name?" He thought for a moment. "Ollie Banghart. I think we put some money in his campaign last year. I'd give anything if this hadn't happened. I was swinging on the duck. I was low to start with. Much too low. When the gun came around, there Walter was, falling toward me. It was too late to do anything."

"Falling?" Shayne said.

Hallam brushed his forehead. "No, he couldn't have been falling. He was coming toward me, his arms out. But why was he there at the front of the blind? He hadn't moved off the bench all morning. I need to sit down." He took a step toward the blind. "No. Not in there."

Shayne summoned young Hallam with a movement of his head. "Take him to the lodge. I'll wait for the sheriff."

"We'd been arguing," Hallam said. "He was intense about it, as usual. Why couldn't I just let it go? Once he got an idea in his head, you couldn't get it out unless you used dynamite." Forbes started to take his arm. He pulled away. "I'm all right. Bring my gun, Shayne."

"Yeah," Shayne said, and watched them go off across the marsh toward the road.

When they were out of sight, he stepped into the blind again and studied the body, checking the angle of the shot. The flies were already gathering. Shayne took off his canvas hunting vest and spread it over the bloody head.

He returned outside and lit a cigarette. The tide was going. He heard a rustle of wings overhead and a shotgun banged in the last blind, off by itself a quarter mile to the south.

Half an hour passed. Finally a car came down the gravel road, traveling very fast, and skidded to a stop. Three men got out. They were all heavily built, and at that distance they looked somewhat alike, but it was easy to see that the man in the middle was the sheriff.

Shayne walked into a constrained silence in the lodge an hour later. It was a low, unpretentious building of split cypress logs, one large central room separating the kitchen from a bunkhouse. Shayne took a quick head count. Begley was still missing.

The senior Hallam, in a chair in front of the big fireplace, was intent on a crossword puzzle. Shayne went over to him.

"I'd like to see you outside for a minute."

Hallam looked up. After a pause, he completed lettering the word he had begun. Then he crumpled the newspaper and threw it in the fireplace.

"Where's the sheriff?"

"He'll be along in a minute."

They went outside and got into one of the two open jeeps. Hallam's normal color had returned, but he still gave the appearance of being so wound up that a touch would send him spinning out of control.

"What did the sheriff have to say?"

"Not much," Shayne told him, "and he took his time about saying it. He's a slow talker."

"Yes, Ollie's slow."

"He'll want to take you through it step by step, but I can't waste that much time. What were you and Langhorne arguing about?"

Hallam gripped the wheel in both hands. "The usual thing. The way I run the company. We've had the same argument at two-week intervals for fifteen years."

"Specifically."

Hallam hesitated. "He didn't like the idea of taking the T-239 investigation outside the company. The whole thing is my fault, for not moving into production on the strength of the preliminary tests. That was a hard decision to make. But if I'd hurried, if trouble had developed later, the board would have been justified in asking for my resignation. Walter worked himself up to quite a pitch. Finally, for the nth time, he told me he was quitting. I made some slighting comment, and then the duck came over. When I brought the gun around, there he was in front of me."

"Was he drunk?"

Hallam moved his head. "You couldn't tell with Walter. His speech wasn't slurred or heavy."

"Will you try to remember what you said just before he jumped? It might be important."

Hallam reflected. "It had something to do with you. I believe I said to wait till we found out if you deserved your reputation. Something like that."

"Do you think he's the one who passed the paint material to Begley?"

Hallam turned his head sharply. "Certainly not."

"Forbes doesn't think it's impossible."

"Forbes doesn't know what he's talking about!" Hallam snapped.

"Were you told that Langhorne had been dickering with Candida Morse of the Begley firm?"

"What do you mean, 'dickering'? They were seen together once, at a sort of party. We don't know who initiated it or what was said. I don't condemn a man on that kind of evidence."

"How was he fixed for money?"

Hallam shrugged. "We paid him a good salary. He had no one to spend it on but himself. And it always seemed to me that he kept getting small inheritances from various aunts. He never talked about the vulgar subject. That's usually a tipoff that somebody's not suffering."

"You've been living with this thing for several months now. If you don't think Langhorne did it, do you suspect anybody else?"

"I suspect everybody. That's the damnable thing. Everybody suspects everybody. This has opened a real fissure in the company, and we won't be able to close it until we find out who's actually guilty."

"Forbes said he was beginning to suspect himself. I don't think he was serious. What do you think of the possibility?"

At his son's name, Hallam's arm jerked and the horn blared. "Excuse me. I don't think much of it. He'll inherit fifty percent of my stock. He'd be going against his own interests. I don't want to close off any legitimate inquiry, but you'd be throwing away your time pursuing that one. I suppose he meant he had the opportunity. So did fifteen or twenty other people. You'd better sit down and have a talk with Miss McGonigle, our counterintelligence department."

"That's the first thing I'd do if I had time," Shayne said. "But if I'm going to come up with anything between now and Monday, I'll have to work on it from the other end."

"By that you mean Begley?"

"Begley's firm. He didn't break out of the small time until Candida Morse went to work for him. She's the brains of the combination. And Begley's going to be out of contention all day, probably into tomorrow. As a rule, he's a fairly cool drinker. His strategy for the weekend is to get drunk and stay drunk, so nobody can ask him any questions."

"You know your business," Hallam said doubtfully. "But if you simply go to this Morse woman and ask her who she was dealing with at Despard's, why should she tell you anything?"

Shayne's eyes were hard. "That's not the way I'll do it. I'll push her a little first. We have a small score to settle. It may not work, but I can't see any other way of getting results in a hurry. If there isn't a quick payoff, I'll come to the office Monday morning and run a routine credit check on the list of possibilities."

A black Chevrolet appeared, moving fast.

"There's the sheriff. If he talked as fast as he drives, I'd stick around. He'll tie you up most of the day. Is your plane still at the airstrip?"

"Yes. Use it if you want to. Some of the others may want to go back at the same time."

The Chevy went into a long screeching skid in front of the lodge.

Shayne said, "Do you think there's any chance Langhorne committed suicide?"

"Suicide?"

"He did everything but throw himself on your gun. People sometimes have scruples against killing themselves, and get somebody else to do it for them. It's not unknown."

Hallam squinted at the approaching sheriff. He didn't answer.

Shayne went on, watching him, "And there's a third possibility. Homicide."

Hallam's knuckles were white on the steering wheel. "I think I see what you're trying to do, Shayne, prepare me for my morning with the sheriff. But I doubt if Ollie Banghart will want to open up that area. You're wondering if Walter admitted selling us out and I lost control and shot him. The answer, for the record, is no. It's true that I identify myself closely with the interests of my company, but anyone will tell you I am not what you would call a passionate man."

CHAPTER 4

At 6:30 that evening, the phone clanged in Michael Shayne's Buick. Shayne and his friend Tim Rourke, a reporter on the *Miami News,* were parked in front of a fire plug on Biscayne Boulevard, talking quietly. Rourke had a big square Speed Graphic camera on his lap. He was slumped deep in his seat with his bony knees up against the dashboard. Extremely thin, unshaven, his clothes wrinkled and spotted, he gave no indication that he was actually extremely hardworking and very difficult to fool. He had won one Pulitzer Prize for local reporting and had been cited three other years, usually in connection with stories he had worked on with Shayne.

Shayne picked up the phone.

"Teddy Sparrow," a voice said. "The Morse dame. She's having dinner at Larue's with a date."

"Who's the man?" Shayne asked.

"I never saw him before, Mike. He hasn't got much of a tan. Good clothes—I think he'd be tanned if he lived here year-round. He's driving a Hertz Chevy. I peeked at the card on the steering column."

"Good, Teddy. Wait there. I'll be with you in five minutes."

He hung up and started the motor. Rourke dropped his cigarette to the floor and ground it out.

"How hammy do you want this to be, Mike? I take it the girl isn't too stupid."

"She's probably smarter than both of us put together. We're not trying to fool her. This is pressure."

"The funny thing is," the reporter said thoughtfully, "it would actually make a very nice series. These headhunters haven't had much publicity yet. There's a couple of others in town besides Begley. Miami's logical place. A guy can come down and a personnel man can meet him. It's really a job interview, but the theory is that everybody's just on vacation."

Shayne drove south on the Boulevard, turning left after a dozen blocks to a long ramp which took him onto the MacArthur Causeway. Halfway across the bay, he dropped onto Poinsettia Island and parked near a small French restaurant that had recently opened there, with a long private dock for customers who came by boat from the Miami Beach marinas.

Teddy Sparrow shambled up as Shayne got out. He was a mountainous, hopelessly inept private detective who seldom handled anything except open-and-shut divorces or tracer jobs for collection agencies.

"They got their table, Mike. They had one martini at the bar, one at the table. How do we handle this?"

"I handle it, Teddy," Shayne said. "She'll probably come out alone. See where she goes. She may have spotted you by now, but that's not too important. Just don't lose her."

"I don't get flimflammed too often," the other detective said confidently. "Then I call you on the car phone, right?"

"Right."

"I wish I had one of those phones in my car," Sparrow said wistfully. "Throw me some more business, Mike, and damn if I won't put my name on the waiting list."

Shayne and Rourke entered the restaurant. "What's the name of the maître?" Shayne said. "George, isn't it?"

"Hell, no!" Rourke said, shocked. "Albert. Imagine forgetting anything that important. You could end up at a table next to the kitchen."

A dark man in a tuxedo came out of the crowd that was overflowing from a small bar.

"Mr. Shayne!" he exclaimed, glad to have the well-known detective to dress up his room. "A table. Certainly." He looked at Rourke with less enthusiasm. "For two?"

"Not right now—Albert," Shayne said. "You know Tim Rourke, don't you? Of the *News.*"

"Of course," Albert said with more warmth.

"We won't give you any trouble," Shayne said. "We want to get a picture. If the paper uses it, Larue's will be mentioned."

"Whatever you wish, Mr. Shayne. And if you could mention the location? Poinsettia Island."

Shayne explained what they wanted while Rourke shut himself in a public phone booth and dialed Larue's number. The phone rang in an alcove between the bar and the main dining room. After answering, Albert dispatched a waiter to tell Candida Morse that she had a phone call from Pride's Landing, Georgia.

Shayne, meanwhile, worked his way through the crowd in the bar. He came out at the far end as Candida Morse crossed the room and picked up the phone.

She had been given one of the desirable tables on the glassed-in terrace, with a view of the lights of downtown Miami. The man she was with had close-cut hair and black-rimmed glasses. He seemed pleased with himself. There was a tiny American Legion pin in his buttonhole. He was somewhat overweight, but expensive clothes took care of the problem. He was thinking pleasant thoughts as he fingered his martini, which had been served on the rocks in an old-fashioned glass.

His eyes met Shayne's as the detective passed his table. Their eyes held for an instant. Shayne gave him a half-nod of recognition, then turned back after a step and studied his face.

"Your name wouldn't be Stanley Woodward, by any chance?"

The other man smiled. "Case of mistaken identity. Sorry."

"From New York," Shayne said. "Stanley J. Woodward. Cashier, Guaranty Trust Co. Butch haircut, horn-rims, always has an American Legion insignia in his buttonhole."

The man glanced down humorously at his own buttonhole. "You're barking up the wrong tree, I assure you."

"For your sake I hope so," Shayne grated, "because the man I'm thinking of beat his bank out of forty-odd thousand in cash." He flipped open his leather folder to give the man a fast glimpse of his private detective's license. "Your identification, please."

"Look here—" the man started to protest, but broke off and took out his wallet. "Driver's registration. Diner's Club. Social Security card. Take your pick."

Shayne looked at the data on the Missouri driver's registration. The man's name was Clark Ahlman. He lived in St. Louis, where he worked for a large lead company.

"I may have made a mistake, Mr. Ahlman," he said more politely. "That's the trouble with these condensed descriptions—they fit too many people. That American Legion button did it."

"No harm done," Ahlman said. "I'm sorry to hear a fellow Legionnaire's an embezzler."

"It's Michael Shayne," Candida's voice said coolly at Shayne's elbow. "The line was dead, which seemed odd. Now I understand it. You two know each other?"

"We just met this minute," Shayne said cheerfully, returning Ahlman's wallet.

He stepped aside. Tim Rourke, who had followed Candida back through the dining room, crouched with the big Speed Graphic to his eye and shot a picture of Ahlman pulling out her chair so the girl could sit down. She was wearing a low-cut black dinner dress. The exploding flashbulb caught her with an expression Shayne had never seen her without: cool, withdrawn, faintly amused. It went with her careful makeup and well-groomed hair.

Ahlman said threateningly, scowling, "What is this? What are you people trying to pull?"

"It's on the nature of a practical joke," Candida said, seating herself. "I wouldn't worry about it. I won't introduce you because they aren't staying." She brought a waiter to the table with a flick of her finger. "Will you ask Albert to step out here, please?"

The waiter disappeared.

"Practical joke, hell," Rourke said, unscrewing the blackened flashbulb. "We've been trying for a picture of Candida Morse in action for a couple of weeks. And it wouldn't be any good without the guy's name."

"Candida," Ahlman murmured, "I think on the whole—"

"Sit down, Clark. Mr. Shayne and friend are merely trying to rattle me in connection with something altogether different. We're within the Miami Beach city limits, aren't we, Mr. Shayne? I believe so. And it's well known that you're not popular with the Beach police. I'll call them if you like, but it would be simpler if you just went away. Take Tim Rourke with you."

"We don't seem to be wanted, Mike," Rourke said, grinning. "And I thought she'd like to hear about the series we're running."

"What series?" Ahlman said, alarmed.

He had sat down, but he was using only the front few inches of his chair, unable to imitate Candida's ease of manner.

"I'm on the *News,*" Rourke explained. "We're working up an exposé of industrial-spy outfits that masquerade as executive employment agencies. People are always complaining that I only give one side of the story. I thought I'd give Miss Morse a chance to express her point of view."

Candida shook her head pityingly. "What a hypocrite you are, after all, Mr. Rourke. I know the kind of hatchet job you're capable of. I'm certainly not going to offer the back of my neck."

The waiter appeared and said almost rudely, "Albert had to go out."

Clark Ahlman stood up. "Candida, this isn't anything

that calls for the police. Let's simply cancel our dinner order and go somewhere else."

"They'd come with us, I'm afraid," she said with a smile. "One of the things a private detective and a newspaper reporter have in common is a thick hide. Let's assume our evening is over. I'm sorry. You go on, Clark. I'll call you at the hotel later."

"Are you sure it's O.K.?" he asked, itching to leave. "I mean, I wouldn't want to feel—"

"I'm quite sure. Don't be concerned about me. I eat private detectives like canapés."

Picking up a stalk of celery, she bit into it with a quick crunch of her even white teeth. She held out her hand. Ahlman shook it quickly and went off among the tables, turning to glance back at the entrance.

"Farewell, cowardly lion," Candida said coolly. "Farewell ten-percent commission. When I call his hotel, I'm afraid I'll be told he's already checked out. Are you really doing a piece on us, Mr. Rourke?"

"Thinking about it," he said, grinning. "But Mike's been telling me that if I do it his way, I could end up with something bigger. He's usually right." He flicked a hand at the detective. "That gets rid of the guy, and I've got to take off. See you, pal."

"Sit down," Candida said. "This is an expense-account evening. I'll buy you both dinner."

"You won't buy me dinner," Rourke said. "I'm due on the other side of town half an hour ago and theoretically I'm supposed to have a clean shave when I get there." He looked her over admiringly. "Baby, you're terrific. I have the feeling I'll see you again. Don't let Mike scare you. He's not as tough as he looks."

"You'll join me, won't you, Mr. Shayne?" she said, giving Shayne a slanting upward look as Rourke walked away. "You can eat Mr. Ahlman's dinner."

Shayne moved the table and slid into the unoccupied chair. "What's he having?"

"Crabmeat thermidor. It's supposed to be quite good here."

Albert loomed up at the other side of the table to find out if everything was satisfactory.

"I was told you went out," Candida said icily.

"For a minute," Albert told her without embarrassment. "Would you care to order dinner, Mr. Shayne?"

"I'm having the crabmeat that's already ordered," Shayne said. "Send me a double cognac in a wine glass. Miss Morse, another martini?"

"I'll wait for the wine." When they were alone, she said to Shayne, "It would be stupid, wouldn't it, after all we went through in that Pittsburgh Plate Glass business, not to use our first names?"

Shayne shrugged. "All right with me."

"I caught a glimpse of Teddy Sparrow in my rearview mirror. I suppose that was your doing?"

"I thought you'd probably spot him."

"That was the idea, wasn't it, so I'd know I was being chivvied? We used Teddy for a small job once. Never again. I suppose I can look forward to the pleasure of his company for an indefinite period?"

"The client's paying for it."

"And who is your client, Mike?"

"Despard's. You know that."

"I suspected as much. Have they lost something valuable?"

Her lips moved at the corners. She was leaning toward him slightly, her eyes alive. A bracelet sparkled as she revolved her martini glass. She had set out to charm him, and she obviously thought it was going to be easy. He decided to remove her smile.

"Walter Langhorne's dead."

The smile went. He was looking into her eyes, and he thought the shock there was real.

"Walter."

"Hallam shot him in the face with a twenty-gauge shotgun at pointblank range."

The blood drained out of her face. Her eyes rolled upward, which gave her the look of falling forward. Then she actually did fall. He shot an arm in front of her to take her opposite shoulder, catching her before she was too far out of balance. From other parts of the terrace, heads swung toward them. Candida's blonde hair partially concealed her face.

"Sir? Is anything wrong with the lady?"

It was the waiter, bringing Shayne's cognac. Still gripping the girl's shoulder, most of her weight on his forearm, Shayne reached over his own arm and fished an ice cube out of one of the water glasses.

"She's out cold!" the waiter exclaimed.

"Yeah."

Shayne pressed the ice against the soft flesh behind the lobe of Candida's ear. As the ice melted, the cold water ran along her jawline and down her neck. She shivered. When her shoulder tightened under his hand, he let her go.

Her head continued forward a few inches, but she snapped the rest of the way out of her faint before she hit the table. Pushing back her hair, she looked from face to face, ending at Shayne's. The intelligence was back in her eyes.

"I fainted." She made it an accusation.

"Yeah, probably for the first time in your life," he said. "Anybody can see you're not the swooning type. If that was a fake, it was a good one. More cognac," he told the waiter. "Two doubles. Here."

He held the glass to the girl's bloodless lips. Taking it from him, she drained it in one long pull and breathed out with a cough. Although still pale, she was nearly back to normal.

"You believe in body-punching, don't you, Mike? That really jarred me. You must know I've been seeing Walter, or you wouldn't have done it that way."

"It's almost the only thing I do know," Shayne said. "Young Hallam told me somebody saw you together at an art auction in Palm Beach. I didn't think it meant anything. If you'd wanted not to be seen, you could have fixed something."

"Don't forget the law of averages, Mike. It's too small a world." She drew another long breath. "I'm sorry about Walter."

"Another lost commission."

She gave him a straight look and said in a level voice, "There was no question of a commission. He'd already decided to stay where he was. You caught me off balance, but I'm beginning to ask myself a few questions. You wanted to scare me into thinking Hallam shot him because of his meetings with me. I don't believe it. That was a typical duck-shooting weekend—whiskey and loaded shotguns. It was an accident, of course."

"Maybe," Shayne said briefly.

The waiter brought two more cognacs. Candida shook her head when he put one in front of her, and slid it toward Shayne. The detective drank.

He went on, "What were you talking to Langhorne about at that auction—a higher-paying job with some other company, or a new kind of paint? I thought I might find out if I sprung it on you. It hadn't occurred to me that you might actually like him."

"I liked him."

"All right. You'll hear about it from Begley as soon as he's sober. The senior Hallam and Langhorne were alone in a two-man shooting blind. Hallam's a big taxpayer in that part of the world. He knows the sheriff's first name. I think it's probably gone in as an accidental shooting. But there are a couple of odds and ends you may want to know about. Langhorne had Scotch for breakfast this morning. If his flask was full when he started out, he drank nearly a pint between four-thirty and seven. The first thing the sheriff was going to do when he got the body to town was get an alcohol count. Hallam said they'd been arguing. If I'd done a little hammering in the first five minutes, I think he would have given it to me word for word. That was another thing I didn't think was important. He was having second thoughts when we talked later. By that time it didn't sound much like a shooting argument. What he was really doing was rehearsing his story for the sheriff. When he talked to the sheriff, he probably stepped it down another notch."

"Why do you say that this concerns me?"

"A man's been killed, Candida," Shayne said patiently. "That always makes a difference."

He swung around so he could bear down on her. "Up to now I'm sure it's all been wonderful fun. You have an adventurous job. You've been making money, eating in good restaurants, meeting fascinating men from St. Louis, setting up clandestine deals. Here's the other side, all of a sudden. Who's really responsible for Langhorne's death? You are."

"Mike, you're raving," she said uneasily.

"Hallam's finger pulled the trigger. That's the only thing there's no doubt about. He kept making a funny remark. He said Langhorne fell toward the gun. Did Langhorne deliberately put himself in the way of the shot? Was the quarrel so tense and upsetting that they both forgot the loaded shotgun? Or did Hallam provoke it, to get Langhorne to rush him? I saw the duck go over. There was something wrong about the angle. Hallam should have been shooting more to the left, unless the gun went off before it was all the way to his shoulder. Those are the main possibilities, and you're mixed up in every one of them."

"What are you talking about?"

"Maybe your name wasn't mentioned," Shayne said softly, "but they were fighting about you. You haven't started to think about it. If he was only a suit of clothes to you, you won't be bothered by any of this. I doubt if you're that far gone."

"Mike, outside of trying to make me feel like a heel, what do you want from me, exactly?"

"Begley drew a hundred and twenty G's from United States Chemical during the spring and summer. We assume that was payment for the transfer of a three-hundred-page report on a new paint developed by my client. I want to know who supplied that report and how much he was paid. If you pried it out of him for nothing, I want to know what you used as a handle."

"That's all."

He grinned at her. "For openers. And I'd really like to put your boss in jail. That may not be possible this time, but if it isn't I'll keep trying."

"Mike, you keep shifting ground. There are certain conceivable admissions Hal might make, but not at the point of a gun."

"I don't agree with you," Shayne said. "That's the only way to get him to do anything. You know him better than I do. How much pressure do you think he can stand?"

"I don't think it'll come to that. We're in good shape on this, it seems to me. You've had a salutary effect on us, Mike. We've toned up our procedures. If you ever manage to subpoena our records again, you'll find everything in order. On this consultant job for United States, we have the correspondence and a work schedule, and I don't believe the courts would consider our fee excessive. What you can do in the way of pressure, if you're willing to spend money, is scare off a few potential clients, like poor Clark Ahlman, who naturally don't want their present employers to know they're looking for a job somewhere else. I don't think Hal will let himself be intimidated. In fact, we may close down the office temporarily and take a vacation."

"When you come back, don't open up in Miami."

"The hell with you, Mike Shayne!" she said abruptly, pushing back her chair. "If you're going in for low punching, you'd better get ready to take a few yourself. Hal wanted me to feel you out on a possible deal. I talked him out of it. I knew you wouldn't be open to any reasonable arrangement. Tell Tim Rourke to have his lawyers check anything he prints for libel. We'd love to bring that kind of suit. Win or lose, the publicity would be divine."

Shayne stopped her momentarily by saying in an amused voice, "How old are you, Candida?"

She made an angry exclamation, threw down her napkin like a grenade and stood up. She ignored the waiter, who was arriving with a large tray.

"The lady?" the waiter said, looking after her retreating back. "Doesn't she want her dinner?"

"What did she order?" Shayne asked.

"Veal in caper sauce. Very nice tonight."

"Leave it," Shayne said. "I'm hungry."

CHAPTER 5

Shayne sent back the wine Candida had ordered and asked for another cognac. He was having his second cup of coffee after finishing the two meals when Albert, the maître d', hurried toward him.

"Mr. Shayne, is that your Buick in the parking lot? The black sedan? The phone's ringing in it."

Shayne dropped several bills on the table to cover the check. He heard the muffled ringing of the phone as he strode rapidly toward his Buick. Pulling open the door, he snatched up the phone and said hello.

There was no answer, but the kind of noises he heard told him he had caught the call in time; he had a live connection.

"Hello?" he said again. "Mike Shayne speaking."

This time there was a low, vaguely human mumble.

"Say it again," Shayne said carefully. "Closer to the phone."

"Ehh—"

It was little more than a groan, but when it was repeated Shayne recognized the voice that made it.

"Teddy? O.K. Where are you?"

Several deep breaths were taken at the other end of the connection while Sparrow gathered enough strength to bring out a word. It sounded like, "Woodlawn."

"Woodlawn Cemetery?" Shayne said. "Yes or no."

He was answered by a slurred vowel sound, an affirmative.

"I'll make it as fast as I can," Shayne said.

He swore savagely as he slammed down the phone and switched on the ignition. He reversed and came down on the gas hard, leaving twin smears of rubber on the blacktop. He swung out of the parking area with most of the Buick's weight on the two inside wheels.

On the causeway, he settled down to some serious driving, part of the time on the wrong side of the double line. He took the Boulevard south to 8th Street, then went straight out 8th until he reached the big cemetery in Southwest Miami.

The main gates were locked. He cruised along the tall iron fence. On 32nd Avenue, across from Coral Park, he saw a lighted phone booth. It seemed empty at first. The door was closed, and he was almost past when he perceived that something was jammed against it from the inside.

Bringing the Buick to a stop, he leaped out. The phone dangled to within an inch or two of Teddy's misshapen felt hat. The hat was rammed down over his forehead. His heavy body completely filled the bottom quarter of the booth, as though stuffed into it forcibly from above.

Shayne tried to open the door, but with Teddy's two hundred and sixty pounds jammed against the center fold, he moved it only an inch.

"Teddy!" he snapped. "Can you hear me?"

The shapeless bulk didn't stir.

Noises were coming from the dangling phone. Shayne put his full weight against the door, producing enough of an opening to admit an arm. He managed to grasp Teddy's jacket. He yanked at the unconscious figure, synchronizing his pulls with increased pressure on the door. He gave up after a moment. There was only one way to get Teddy out, and that was to pry off the door.

He unlocked the Buick's trunk and brought out the jackhandle, one end of which was flattened so it could be used on hubcaps. Shayne forced the flat end into the crack between the folding door and the frame of the booth, and leaned against it. The thinner metal of the door creaked and began to bend.

This was a quiet part of town. So far no cars had passed. One was approaching now, but Shayne went on with what he was doing. A screw popped.

The car slowed. It had a noisy motor and a noisier muffler.

A voice called above the racket, "Stealing dimes out of the phone?"

Shayne glanced around. There were three men in the front seat of a dirty cream-colored Plymouth. The speaker was a youth of eighteen or nineteen, with his hair in his eyes. The visible portions of his face were marred with patches of acne.

"Man passed out in here," Shayne grunted. "The door has to come off."

The boy stepped out. He proved to be six feet two or three, and looked as though he had been put on a rack and stretched.

"Give you a hand, hey. Nothing like breaking up telephone-company property. Whitey, there's a tire tool on the floor. Let's help the man."

Leaving the motor running, the driver got out and felt under the front seat. He was stocky and muscular, with pale skin and hair and eyebrows so white he was nearly an albino.

"I'm coming along fine, thanks," Shayne said. "On your way, boys."

The long-haired youth stepped on the sidewalk, making a point of looking into the phone booth instead of at Shayne.

"Can't we even watch?"

The third man, a heavy-set pockmarked Cuban, slid over and swung his legs out of the car but remained seated. He was older than the other two, with graying hair and sad cow's eyes. The stump of a cigar was clamped between his jaws.

"Passed out?" the youth said, peering in at Sparrow. "Clobbered out is more like it. Big—no wonder the door won't open. How about breaking the glass?"

He turned toward Shayne to ask the question. Shayne had been in circulation long enough to know there had to be a reason for three such dissimilar people to be cruising the streets in that kind of car, and he brought the jack-handle down and around to meet the youth as he drove in at Shayne's midsection with a fist armed with brass knuckles.

The knuckles glanced off the steel handle. Shayne continued the stroke with a vicious cut at the youth's head. He missed by inches.

The follow-through carried them into a hard collision. Shayne swung one leg at the hinge of the boy's knees, bringing his elbow up hard. He wanted to get this one out of the way fast, before he had to meet the other two.

He felt and heard the crunch of cartilage as the youth's nose was flattened against his face. Tripped by Shayne's swinging leg, he was already on his way down. Shayne's knee came up to meet him. He went over backward, arms and legs splaying in four directions. Blood spurted from the mess that had been his nose.

The Cuban was out of the car, moving fast. Shayne had one more thing to take care of. He had a bias against people who swung on him with brass knuckles. The boy's hand, palm upward, scraped the sidewalk as he fought to recover. Shayne's heel came down hard and the boy screamed.

Shayne was already turning to meet the Cuban's rush.

The Cuban dived beneath the jackhandle, grabbing the detective around the thighs. Whitey was running around the front of the car, a short taped club in one hand, probably the meat end of a baseball bat. Shayne was driving, and the Cuban couldn't hold him. Shayne swung the jackhandle. Whitey pirouetted away like a dancer.

Shayne staggered and nearly fell. Recovering, he jabbed the flat end of the handle downward twice at the Cuban's kidneys. The Cuban's grip on his waist loosened and Shayne twisted free.

Whitey was now at the inner edge of the sidewalk, Shayne at the curb. Whitey darted in, faked a swing at Shayne's knees, then struck upward, sending the jackhandle spinning out of Shayne's hand.

Shayne gathered up the Cuban and whirled him at his companion. The Cuban caromed off and hit the phone booth with such force that one of the corner uprights folded inward. Shayne ducked a whistling blow from the club and caught a second on his forearm.

The youth on the sidewalk flung himself on Shayne from behind. Shayne fell. He began his roll even before he hit the sidewalk. The Cuban landed on him. Shayne struggled to throw him off while Whitey stamped around the edges waiting for a shot at Shayne's head. The tall long-haired youth was also part of the melee but not doing much damage. The Cuban butted upward, and the top of his head collided with the knockout point in front of Shayne's ear. The detective was hurt for the first time.

The bat descended. Whitey was trying to connect with a short slashing blow to make Shayne hold still for the real one to follow. Shayne saw the moving shadow and jerked aside. The club hit the Cuban. Shayne came into a crouch, bringing the dazed Cuban up with his left hand. He brought him around against the iron pickets of the cemetery fence, nailing him with a powerful right as he hung there. The click as it landed told him the Cuban was through for the night.

He looked for Whitey, who turned as Shayne turned. The club was already on its way down. Shayne slanted upward to meet it, and the club slammed him across the back of the neck.

"You got him!" the youth cried. "You got the bastard. Spill his brains on the sidewalk."

Whitey growled, "Back in the car."

"Back in the car! Look at my hand. Give me that."

"This is Mike Shayne, meathead. Did Jake say to kill him? We didn't get paid that kind of dough."

Shayne lay face down, his knees in the gutter. He could hear the voices, but the words were unclear. The Plymouth's motor panted noisily beside him. Unconsumed gases washed over him from the leaking muffler. The blow at the top of the spine had cut his communication with his arms and legs. He strained to move. He could feel drops of sweat break out on his forehead. Willing his shoulders into motion, he lifted his head a few inches.

Whitey dragged the unconscious Cuban past and thrust him into the car. The boy, one arm dangling, kept on begging for the club.

"Just one lick!"

"Leave him be, goddamn it," Whitey snarled. "In the car, in the car!"

Shayne raised his head another inch and sank his teeth in the boy's ankle.

The boy was wearing white jeans with pipe-stem legs, which stopped halfway down his calves. Shayne bit down hard, trying to sever the Achilles tendon. The boy gave a high bubbly cry.

"Will you come on?" Whitey cried. "I said to leave him alone!"

With a choked obscenity, the youth took a step and snatched up the jackhandle. Whitey grabbed his arm as it came down. Shayne's teeth unclenched and he rolled out of the way. His arms and legs were answering now, but sluggishly.

The youth pulled out of Whitey's hands and ran to the driver's side. The door there was open. He leaped in. Whitey wrenched the door open on the near side as the car careened recklessly backward. Twenty yards away it reversed and came back at Shayne.

The detective commanded his body to roll, but he could count the seconds before the movement started. The youth with his one usable hand and Whitey with two fought for control of the wheel. The Plymouth swerved, mounting the curb, then rocked back to the street before veering onto the sidewalk again. Shayne, his head on a level with the front bumper, saw the wheels begin to turn toward the street, but in one frozen quarter-second he could see that the correction wouldn't be made in time. He struggled to bring his arm against his body. The car whooshed past, and he felt a blazing pain in his forearm.

There was a rending crash. The Plymouth's front fender hooked the phone booth and knocked it over.

The car bounced away, swung all the way across the street and shuddered to a stop. Whitey burst out of the front seat and ran around to take the wheel.

Hitching forward in a crablike crawl, Shayne reached the overturned booth. The Plymouth starter was growling.

Shayne wrestled himself around, braced his feet against the booth and began to pull Teddy out through the bottom.

It was painful work, and he was no longer really sure what he was doing.

The Plymouth's sudden stop had flooded the carburetor. The starter ground on and on, beginning to weaken. The open phone in the overturned booth buzzed and crackled, and Teddy moaned. Amid the confusion of noises Shayne thought he heard a siren.

The carburetor cleared and the motor took hold with a roar. Black smoke billowed from the exhaust. Shayne gave up the attempt to free Teddy and crawled in with him, pulling open his jacket. His hand fastened on the butt of the .38 in the shoulder holster.

The gun resisted. The Plymouth wheeled over the opposite curb and moved away, accelerating. Shayne fought the .38. Apparently the holster had a security spring to keep the gun from being drawn by anyone else but the wearer.

He changed his grip. The gun jumped into his hand and he fired without aiming.

The Plymouth was rounding the corner into 16th Street. Shayne's snap shot blew out a rear tire. The back end careered through a ninety-degree arc and smashed against a utility pole.

Shayne fired again, aiming carefully, and drilled a hole through the safety glass in front of the driver. Whitey understood the message, and stayed where he was.

Shayne propped the gun on the large man's buttocks, holding the front sight steady on the thug's unnaturally white hair. He was in the same position when the police arrived. He still had the gun in an iron grip, and pressure on the trigger would have sent a slug through Whitey's head. But Shayne was unconscious.

CHAPTER 6

The casualties were taken to Jackson Memorial, across the river on 12th Avenue.

The doctor on emergency duty when Shayne was carried in was an old-timer named Hugo Baumgartner, who had worked on him before. In addition to a lacerated ear and various contusions, Shayne's main problem was his smashed left wrist. Baumgartner set the bones. After studying his work in hastily developed X rays, he rebroke them and did it again. When Shayne fought his way out of the anesthetic, Baumgartner was tidying up after putting on a light finger-tip-length cast.

He looked at the detective solemnly. His face had long ago congealed in this expression; Shayne had never seen him smile.

"They hit you with a car this time, I'm sorry to see."

"Where's Sparrow?"

"Upstairs asleep. Kind of funny thing happened. Want to hear it?"

"I need a laugh."

"He got out of bed when the nurse wasn't looking. He didn't know it was a hospital bed. He broke an ankle. Kind of complicated. His right leg's in traction."

"Yeah, that's funny," Shayne agreed, deadpan.

"I thought so. His speech and vision are O.K., but we have to wait till tomorrow to see about brain damage from the beating. Of course somebody who knows Sparrow tells me not to worry—you couldn't tell the difference. Mike, I didn't want to put on the final before I conferred with you. You've got a tricky fracture. If you want to regain the use of that wrist you have to be careful with it."

"I'm always careful."

"Yes-s," Baumgartner said skeptically. "I know that telling a bank clerk to be careful isn't the same thing as telling Mike Shayne to be careful. I was wondering. How would you like the same kind of cast I gave you the last time? As I remember, I put a sash-weight in the plaster and you broke a guy's jaw with it."

"Yeah," Shayne said faintly; the pain in his wrist was very bad.

The doctor went on, "Not that you have to worry about catching the three guys who jumped you. They're caught. I've got two of them here, and they won't go anywhere under their own power for a few days. I had to go to the saw to get the brass knuckles off without taking the boy's fingers. The third one's in jail. He was driving a stolen car, to begin with."

He mixed plaster as he talked. "I gave you a shot and you'll be with us at least till tomorrow noon. We want to do a set of spine X rays to see if you've got any nerve injury. And after that you're under orders to stay off your feet for a full twenty-four hours. Will you do that, Mike?"

He waited, but the detective didn't answer.

"You don't seem to be enunciating too well, so I'll answer my own question. No, you won't, not if you're on a case, and I assume you are. So the first thing we're going to do is build an armature around the wrist and pack it with foam rubber. Anchor it on both sides of the break."

He worked in silence for a time. Shayne, already half asleep, no longer felt any pain. When Baumgartner spoke again, the words drifted down to him from a great distance.

"I was going to use a sash weight again, but here's an idea. How about the brass knuckles? They're lightweight. They're lethal. I sawed them in two, and I'll point one half one way and the other half the other. Under a sixteenth of an inch of plaster you'll have a dangerous left hand. You can't use your fingers, so why don't I close the cast at the end and put on a hook? And a scalpel, Mike. I'll lay it on top and slap on enough plaster to hold it. Bang it against something and you'll have yourself an edged weapon. This cast is going down in the annals of medical science."

He was still working when Shayne fell asleep.

It was daylight when Shayne awoke. He tried to lift his left arm to look at his watch. He thought at first someone had strapped that hand to the bed. Then the pain hit him and he blacked out briefly. When he came to, he raised his head from the pillow and looked around.

"And the top of the morning to you, too," Sparrow said sourly from the next bed.

Shayne rolled over. The mountainous private detective was sitting up, his right leg attached to a rig that was attached to a hook in the ceiling. His head was swathed in bandages. Nothing showed but his little eyes, a nose with a large scab on it, and a long cigar.

"A simple little follow job," he commented, the cigar still in his mouth. "A hundred-and-ten-pound blonde. Wouldn't hurt a fly."

"You'll get combat pay," Shayne grated. "Medical expenses plus five bills. How did it happen?"

"Why, that sexy blonde in the low dress suckered me, Mike. That's what happened. Before she came out of Larue's, she did some phoning. Having no bug on the line, I can't quote it to you, but the gist I think I can give you." He tapped cigar ashes into a vase of cut flowers on the table between the beds. "She called a certain small-time rat named Whitey Grabowski."

"The name's familiar."

"She told him to pick up a couple of pugs and meet her in the park across from Woodlawn. Then she got in a cab and rode around till they got themselves organized. When she paid off the cab at that park, something told me. But it was either follow her or lose her, and you told me not to lose her."

"What was wrong with your gun?"

"They hit me before I could get it out. A cop was telling me this morning about finding me in the phone booth, but I don't remember putting in that call to you, Mike. I didn't even know I knew your number without looking it up, and I sure as hell didn't look it up. I think they dialed it for me and left me just about three percent conscious. You were the one they were mainly after."

"Somebody mentioned the name Jake. Does that mean anything?"

"Jake Fitch! When you come right down to it, this ain't a too-big town. Whitey and Jake Fitch, they're a twosome. They take these kinds of assignments. Low-level stuff." He gave a hoarse laugh. "The one thing I regret, I wasn't awake to see it. They tell me you couldn't get in the phone booth so you pushed it over."

"You ought to lose a little weight, Teddy."

"Don't I know it. And look at that." He pointed to a two-pound box of chocolates beside the flowers. "My nutty girl friend. Skinny as a pencil, and she eats more than I do."

Shayne reached for the button to call the nurse. She came in before he pressed it, a dark, pretty girl in the usual semitransparent uniform.

"I need a phone," Shayne growled.

"Uh-uh," she said, shaking her head. "You're supposed to take it easy till noon."

"What time is it now?"

"Twenty to," she admitted.

He snorted, beginning to feel better.

"All right," she said reluctantly. "I'll bring you a phone and you can make one call. Then I have to take your temperature and give you a bath and bring you breakfast."

Shayne grinned at her. He had hopes of being back in action before anybody washed him by hand. She left. He swung his legs over the side of the bed, but before he could dismount, the room whirled and he pitched forward against Sparrow's bed.

"Play it cool, Mike," Teddy told him. "I'd get up and help if I didn't have troubles of my own."

With the help of the hook attached to his cast, Shayne clawed his way back to his own bed and fell in as the nurse returned with a phone.

"The switchboard has a call for you," she said. *"What's the matter?"*

"A little dizzy."

She helped him into position against the pillows. He made a whirling signal with his good hand and she cranked up the head of the bed. As it rose, the objects around him swam back into focus. She plugged in the phone and handed it to him.

"Shayne," he said.

"Oh," a girl's voice said hesitantly. She sounded young and scared. "Gee, Mr. Shayne, I hope you didn't get banged up too bad."

"Who's this?"

"Nobody. I mean I don't want to tell you my name. This is strictly my own idea. But what do I care? And don't try to keep me talking so you can trace the call."

"You can't trace dial calls," Shayne said. "Say what you have to say and get the hell off the line."

"Well, if I don't watch my step, what happened to you last night will happen to me, only a heck of a lot worse. One of those three fellows, and I'm not going to tell you which, happens to be a good friend of mine. He just did what somebody else said, so why should he go to jail for it and the other persons be walking around as free as the breeze?"

"Yeah," Shayne said. "There's no justice. I already know who hired them. That wasn't meant to be a secret."

"And maybe you don't know as much as you think you do, too. This isn't just last night. I believe in keeping my ears open. People make phone calls after they think other people have gone to sleep. Does the date April twenty-third mean anything to you?"

"No. What happened on April twenty-third?"

"Nothing much. Not a great deal, really. A certain individual got fifty thousand clams from somebody named Bagley or Babcock or something, that's all. Are you digging me, Daddy?"

Shayne pushed himself up in the bed. "Go on."

"I thought you'd be interested. I don't know can I trust you, is the trouble. If I give you some information, will you promise you won't bring charges against those three guys last night?"

"Sure, you can have all three. I'll gift-wrap them for you."

"And your friend," she said suspiciously, "the fat one, will he make the same deal? Huh?"

"He's right here. I'll ask him." Shayne looked across at Teddy. Without covering the mouthpiece he said, "A girl wants to know what you're planning to do about the assault last night, anything?"

"Forget it," Sparrow said promptly, taking the cigar out of his mouth. "I'm supposed to be able to take care of myself. What kind of image do I come out with if I go bawling to the cops? If anybody asks me, it was too dark to see who was doing what."

"Did you hear that?" Shayne said into the phone. "Do you want me to put him on?"

"I guess not," she said doubtfully. "How do I know you won't say one thing now and do something different later?"

"Let me think about it," Shayne said. "Do you want to come here?"

"To the hospital? Are you crazy or something? These people don't kid, or didn't you realize that yet? Tonight. After dark. I wouldn't set foot anywhere near that hospital. If you're still in, we'll have to make it tomorrow."

"You name the place and time. Before we go any farther, you'd better understand that all I can control is the assault rap. They were driving a stolen car. If you want to make an arrangement on that, you have to make it with the D. A."

She gave a faint moan. "I wouldn't know how to begin. I thought you could—"

"I can put in a recommendation. They don't always do what I tell them."

"Damn it! I didn't think they'd pay attention to a little thing like a car when they can get somebody for murder."

"As far as I know," Shayne said with no change of expression, "nobody's been murdered."

"That shows what an expert *you* are. That's my last word on the subject."

Shayne scraped a thumbnail across the reddish stubble on his jaw. "How would this be? I'll make a statement for the six-o'clock news, strong enough so I can't pull it back tomorrow without looking dumb. Six o'clock—WTVJ. The boys there owe me a favor. If it doesn't sound good enough, don't show up. Where do you want me to meet you and when?"

She swallowed. "I wish I knew how to do this!" After another long hesitation, she poured it out in a quick rush. "Eight o'clock. In Buena Vista. Four ninety-seven Bayview Drive. Apartment nine C."

"Wait a minute."

Shayne snapped his fingers at Sparrow, and the other detective tossed him a ballpoint pen. Shayne had the girl repeat the address, and he wrote it on his cast.

"At eight," she said. "Now listen. Ring the bell just once,

longer than you would usually. But not too long! If I don't happen to be alone, I don't want the other person to think it's funny. Eight on the button, so I'll know it's you. When I buzz for the door, I'll give one long buzz if it's O.K. One buzz, come up. Three or four short buzzes, *don't*. Get sort of lost. I'll come out as soon as I can. I'll stand on the front doorstep and fix my stockings so you'll know it's me. God, I'm scared."

She clattered the phone back on the hook. At the other end of the broken connection, Shayne scraped his jaw thoughtfully with the phone before putting it down.

"That's one difference between me and you," Sparrow observed. "When I'm on a case, I can sit looking at the phone for days and days, and nobody calls me."

"Something phony about this," Shayne said, the thoughtful look still on his face. "I think somebody's trying to sandbag me. I don't like that to happen two days in a row."

CHAPTER 7

Shayne wasted the afternoon on the phone.

In Georgia, he learned from Jose Despard, the coroner, who also delivered the rural mail, had certified the death of Walter Langhorne as one of those unfortunate accidents that are more or less bound to happen if people insist on going shooting with a flask of Scotch after only two hours sleep. Despard sounded tired and hungover.

"It was a rough day, Shayne. After the sheriff left, Hallam really hit the booze. He's always been hard as nails, but one thing he never used to be is mean. He never was that sure of himself. I want to tell you his days are numbered. If he gets past the next board meeting, I'll have to say he's a wizard."

"He isn't answering his phone."

"He flew to Washington. Taking the company plane, naturally. The rest of us had to wait for a commercial flight back. It's a wild-goose chase, as I tried to tell him. He wants to talk to the Patent Office tomorrow about an infringement action. We don't have a leg to stand on, but he won't believe what the lawyers tell him because he thinks lawyers are one cut lower than garbage collectors. Prior use is the big thing. When we finally, at long, long last, get T-239 in the stores, we'll be lucky if United States doesn't sue *us*."

"Are you serious?"

"No, they wouldn't have the gall. It makes my blood sizzle. I told him, we all told him. When you have a revolutionary product, get it on the market first and ask questions afterward. We didn't know it then, but we surely do know it now, the United States people were working their balls off all summer, excuse the expression. It's a textbook case. Ossified management."

"Despard, did anything particular happen this year on April twenty-third?"

"In what connection? I know Forbes figured the copy went out of the office sometime during the last two weeks in April. I don't see how you could pin it down."

"Who do you think did it?"

"Walter. He'd get my vote because he's dead. If we can accept him, maybe everybody can shut up about it. The hell of it is, I can't really talk myself into it, unless he was some kind of Dr. Jekyll and Mr. Hyde."

The nurse was waiting when Shayne hung up. "Time for your bath, Mr. Shayne," she said firmly.

He grinned at her. "Let me get a few more phone calls out of the way first."

He dialed the WTVJ number and arranged for an interview on the subject of the previous night's altercation. Tim Rourke came in while he was completing the arrangements. The reporter listened open-mouthed.

"Mike," he said sadly after Shayne put the phone down, "are you giving those TV creeps an *interview?* After all you and I have been through?"

"I have to tell a few lies," Shayne told him. "You wouldn't want me to lie to the *News,* would you?"

"Maybe not," his friend said uncertainly, "and I don't know what you're talking about, as usual. Could you use a drink?"

Shayne brightened. "Yeah."

Rourke gave a surreptitious look around and produced a pint of cognac, which he had carried past the front desk in a basket of fruit.

"Booze," Sparrow said with pleasure.

Rourke closed the door so they wouldn't be bothered by hospital personnel and poured drinks all around in paper cups.

"I don't think I'll ask for ice," he said. "They might think we were breaching regulations. Now a small explanation, Mike. The last time I saw you, you were sitting down to dinner with a bosomy blonde, and here you are with your arm in a cast. Did it turn out she knew judo?"

Shayne described what had happened, finishing with an account of the puzzling phone call from the girl.

"It sounds kosher to me," Rourke said. "If you wanted to throw the book at those three baboons, you and Teddy, you could put them away for a year. It gives you something you can use. Tie them to the Begley firm, and you can do some damage. You and I know they use blackmail and muscle, but it might shake up some of their legitimate clients if it came out in the papers. Did you hear what I said?" He repeated, "In the papers! Not on TV. You have to get it in black and white or you don't feel the impact. On TV it's some jerk with bags under his eyes passing on gossip."

"I'm using the TV interview to get a message to the girl," Shayne said. "I still don't know. I had the feeling she was reading her lines from cue cards."

"I'll go with you," Rourke offered. "I've got both arms."

Shayne shook his head. "She's skittish enough as it is. But I think I'll look the place over before dark. Did you get any leads to people who knew Langhorne?"

Rourke felt in all his pockets and produced an envelope

on which he had jotted down a list of names and phone numbers. Replenishing his cup from time to time, Shayne worked his way down the list. The general feeling among Langhorne's friends was that he had been frugal about things he regarded as unimportant, and lived within his income. He had been well liked, and he would be missed.

A new nurse came in as he hung up after the final call. She was stout and red-faced, with a mustache, muscular forearms and a fierce baritone.

"Miss Manners says you won't eat, you won't let yourself be bathed, you're refusing medication. Very well, Mr. Shayne. You want to be fed intravenously, is that it?"

"As a matter of fact," Shayne said, swinging his legs out of bed, "I was just checking out."

CHAPTER 8

From the TV studio Shayne drove to Buena Vista. Shifting was his main problem. He had to hold the wheel with his knees while reaching awkwardly across to the gear panel with his right hand.

He was wearing a light yellow pullover. Dr. Baumgartner's multipurpose cast was surprisingly light, but so bulky that the nurse had had to slit the left sleeve before she could get it on him. He was carrying it in a full sling, with the knot in front where he could reach it in a hurry.

He checked the number written on his cast and found the address the girl had given him. It was one of a line of apartment buildings, concrete and glass slabs. A sign in front announced that a few efficiency apartments were still available, all with terraces. After parking the Buick, Shayne fished in his side pocket for the watch he usually wore on his left wrist. It was ten minutes to six. The news program for which he had taped an exchange of questions and answers would go on in another ten minutes.

There was no doorman. He checked the apartment directory. The 9-C slot was empty.

He was standing at the locked inner door, a key in his hand, when a lady in a flowered dress came in from the court. He gestured ruefully with the key.

"It can't be done with one hand," he said. "When you turn the key, you can't turn the knob. When you turn the knob, you can't turn the key."

"Oh, let me!"

She used her own key and held the door for him. He thanked her and they rode up together. She left the elevator at eight. Shayne went on to nine and looked for 9-C. Here, too, there was no name over the buzzer. He checked the time again; it was a minute after six. If a TV set had been on inside the apartment, he would have heard it through the poorly fitted door. He rang the bell.

There was no answer, and he went to work on the door. He had his regular assortment of lock picking equipment, but for most of it he needed two hands. He forced a succession of flexible shims between the latch and the metal strike-plate, building up the pressure slowly until the latch came back. Then he held the shims with the hook, shifted hands carefully and turned the knob. The hook shifted, digging a long splinter out of the wood.

He entered and turned on the light.

He was surprised to see a room with no curtains or carpets. There was a three-quarter bed, but no other furniture. Even the bed, a simple box spring and mattress, had no bedding except for a cotton mattress cover. There were two naked pillows.

There were signs that the room had been used, however —a filled ashtray on the floor by the bed, several crumpled tissues marked with lipstick, a pack of chewing gum, two empty glasses. Shayne picked up one of the glasses and sniffed at it. It smelled of gin.

Bothered by the gouge he had left in the doorframe, Shayne unwrapped a stick of gum. He found the splinter on the floor. After chewing the stiffness out of a small piece of gum, he pressed it into the raw scar, then pressed the splinter on top of that. Hearing sounds farther down the hall, he let the door click shut.

He snapped off the light and faded out to the little terrace. After a wait of several moments, he came back, turned on the light again and continued his inventory of the almost empty apartment. In the kitchen there was a saucepan, a teaspoon, two dime-store mugs, a jar of powdered coffee, in the bathroom medicine cabinet a jar of aspirin, a single toothbrush and a tube of toothpaste.

He returned to the main room, his forehead furrowed with concentration. He could kill two hours in a neighborhood bar, or go back to his Buick and do some more phoning. Or he could depart completely from the girl's instructions and wait here. Making up his mind abruptly, he took one of the pillows from the bed, turned off the ceiling light and went out to the terrace.

Here he discovered the cramped little apartment's single virtue. The terrace, though not much larger than a seat on a Ferris wheel, had a view across the bay to the strange and interesting shapes of the tourist hotels along Miami Beach. He closed the glass double doors and lit a cigarette. After smoking it, he flicked the butt over the concrete railing and watched its long downward arc end in the water. Then he sat down on the floor, jamming the pillow against the wall behind him.

His wrist was aching. Time went slowly.

At a little after seven he was lying on his back on the concrete, his wrist supported on the doubled pillow, when he heard a key being inserted in a lock. He sat up hurriedly. A door in the apartment opened. The ceiling light came on and two barred rectangles of light fell onto the terrace floor beside him.

"Home sweet home," a man said hoarsely. "What a pad. With his dough he could do better."

He was answered by the same voice Shayne had heard on the phone, the voice of a young girl. "His wife keeps him penned up, practically. He gave me a hundred to buy a couple of chairs, but you know me, Jake. There don't seem to be enough minutes in the day."

She laughed. The man said, "How about a little fresh air in here before we pass out?"

Shayne shifted his weight. Footsteps approached the terrace door. He fingered the outline of the short scalpel under its thin coating of plaster and made ready to jump. The door opened. He saw a hand and arm.

"Deedee baby," the man said, turning back, "start getting ready, will you? We've got time, but let's not slice it too close."

"I said eight on the dot," the girl replied, "and all about how I'd buzz if it was O.K. to come up, so what are we worried about?"

"Because this is Mike Shayne," the man said. "He can make you some fast moves. One against three last night, and you'll notice he won."

"Now you're getting me all goose-bumpy again! Right after you put a couple of hours into calming me down. This is going to blow up on us, I know it. I just know it. I told you how he was on the phone. He smelled something."

"He was woozy, kid. He just came out of the anesthetic. Now shut up unless you want a mouthful of knuckles. Get undressed."

"Jake! Golly, that's what I don't like—all the way down. Couldn't I keep on my pants?"

"No, you couldn't keep on your pants. That's not the idea. Will you hurry it up? I want to get out of here."

"You want to get out of here," she said. "I can understand that, because I want to get out of here."

There were sounds that might have been made by a girl undressing. On the terrace, Shayne eased himself to his feet, cradling the cast in his good arm to quiet the throbbing.

Jake remarked, "What a shape you've got on you for seventeen, no kidding."

"Glad you like me, Daddy," she answered with a mock simper.

"Lie down so I can mark you."

"I guess what has to be has to be," she said, resigned. "But boy, what my girl friend's going to say."

"Who the hell cares?"

"I care, if you want to know. Some things, anybody in her right mind will draw the line."

The mattress sighed.

"No," she said suddenly. "No, I can't! I know I said I would, but when you actually see it—"

"Turn over, damn it."

"Jake, please! The rest of it, all right. The mob at school will think I had a little bad luck. With Mike Shayne involved it could even do me some good. But leave the whip out of it, I mean it. Or I swear I'll get dressed and walk out. I'm a person."

"Deedee," he said caressingly. "How many days did you go to that school the last month? About two. You're over sixteen. They can't make you finish. You know what I said, baby. New York! One night in the slammer. Tomorrow morning they let you out on bail. You jump bail and blow. You get a certain amount of page-one publicity, but not under your real name."

"I suppose you don't think anybody's going to be there with a camera and take my picture?" she said scornfully. "Page one! You said it, I didn't. That kind of thing could stick to me the rest of my life."

"Think of the dough, baby doll! We won't have to scratch and scramble when we get to the big town. Maybe I can buy a piece of a nice bar."

Suddenly there was a sharp cracking sound and a cry of pain. Shayne pulled the door out of his way, his eyes hard and dangerous. A little wristwatch alarm went off in the other room and stopped him.

The girl was sobbing. "What did you have to do that for? It hurt."

"Baby, I'm sorry. But you know yourself—you'll never make any headway if you go back on a deal."

"It's in front."

"That's O.K. Don't rub it, let it bleed. It's half past. I've got to get moving. Stop crying, baby. I'll buy you something nice. You don't think I like using a whip on you, do you?"

"You seemed to."

"I did not. I think you're so great, baby. It didn't hurt much, did it?" He left the bed and crossed the room. "The whip goes in the closet. There's blood on it. They'll find it when they look for your clothes. Now I'm going to run through this one last time."

"Jake, we already rehearsed it so much it's running out of my ears."

"One more time, and then you can relax for half an hour. I don't know another doll in town who could do this, Deedee, I really mean that. One thing I want to change. If he comes in with the light on and sees you, his reflexes are going to take him out of here but fast. After you buzz, stick a Kleenex in the door so it won't close. And go in the john, see. When he rings the bell up here, call to him to come in, you'll be out in a minute."

"Come in, I'll be out in a minute," she said sullenly.

"Yeah. Camilli and the other vice cop will be down the hall in the incinerator closet. Sex with whips is a hot pinch in this town."

"Did you tell them it's going to be Shayne?"

"Now how could I tell them that, baby doll? But the reason I picked Vince Camilli—he and Shayne have been sideswiping each other for years. Shayne won't be able to buy his way out or talk his way out. All I said was I'd heard rumors about this apartment, and I'd check and let him know. He's downstairs now. I'll tell him you're home and ready for business, and to come up and get in the incinerator. Then he'll wait for the first John to show up. That way it don't sound too much like a frame."

"Shayne'll know it's a frame, but excuse me for thinking."

"What Shayne knows and what Shayne don't know is no skin off our ass. Can we hang it on him? In the long run, no, especially after you jump bail. What we do is tie him up for a few days."

"So?"

"So why ask me? There's some kind of deadline."

"Jake, I know you'll say no, but couldn't you leave a dress in the closet, anyway? Just a dress, nothing underneath. Those ghouls on the vice squad! I'll honestly die."

"I could leave you a full change of clothes. And Shayne would make you get dressed while Camilli breaks down the door. That wouldn't be half as good. They'll give you a jacket or something to put on. Keep thinking of money, kid. Oh, and don't forget to mention Josie."

"I don't know when."

"Play it by ear. Maybe going down in the elevator. Shayne's going to want to find out who pulled it on him, you know, and that's when you bring up the name. Kiss me, doll. Honest to Christ, you're gorgeous."

"Jake."

"Think about how it's going to be in New York. Baby, we're going to make it big."

"Gee, Shayne's going to be mad."

"Don't worry. He's got a broken arm. Get on your bicycle. Camilli won't want to lose out on this pinch—he won't wait more than a couple of minutes."

"And if Shayne catches up to me," she said bitterly, "so much the better, huh? More blood, more broken bones. Well, it's lucky I'm young. I can bounce."

"We'll bounce all the way to New York, kid. Jesus, I love your skin. See you."

The door opened and closed. Shayne, on the terrace, heard the girl give a long sigh. The box springs rearranged themselves as she changed position.

He stepped into the doorway.

She was unwrapping a stick of gum. Her long black hair was almost to her shoulders, and her features seemed to be crowded into the center of her face by the abundant hair. She had nice breasts and hips. She was sitting on the edge of the bed in an unbecoming slump, her thin shoulderblades like undeveloped wings. The whip had left a slanting mark across her thighs.

She mashed the gum between her teeth and dropped the

wrapper to the floor. Then she looked up and saw him. Her reaction carried her back against the wall.

"You don't really think anybody's going to take you to New York, do you?" Shayne said.

CHAPTER 9

She swallowed the gum. She looked at him in terror, not able to understand how he had sprung into being in what she had thought was an empty apartment.

"Mike Shayne," she whispered.

Then she uncoiled and bolted for the door.

Shayne reached it at the same moment and let her wrench it open. It struck his solidly planted foot. The doorknob was jolted out of her hand. He swung the cast upward without taking it out of the sling and touched her bare breast with the curved point of the hook. She shivered away.

He slapped her with the back of his hand, using his full strength. She went spinning against the bed and across it, to bang hard against the wall. Her eyes crossed for an instant. She touched her face, then crawled off the bed and across the floor toward him.

"Please. Please, Mr. Shayne. I didn't want to."

When she reached him, he hooked his toe under her chin and flung her over on her back.

"If you were out there, you heard me," she cried as he advanced on her. "I pleaded. I only agreed to do it if I didn't have to go to court."

"We can take our time," Shayne said deliberately. "We won't be raided until a man walks in, and I'm already here. Let's allow half an hour. You can answer a lot of questions in that time."

She looked up from the floor. "I don't know anything."

He threatened her with his foot and she shrank back. "I don't! I wasn't trying to be smart-alecky."

He stripped the mattress cover off the bed and flung it at her. "Put this on."

She was taking quick shallow breaths. "You're going to beat me up, aren't you?"

"I might," he said evenly.

She stood up, watching him, and decided to try something different. She filled her lungs, sucking in her stomach and thrusting her breasts toward him. She rubbed her hands slowly against her thighs.

"If we've got half an hour—"

Shayne went to the closet and took out the long whip.

She said hastily, "I just meant I'd cooperate!"

She pulled the coarse cotton mattress cover around her shoulders and brought it together in front. "Boy, is this ever unsexy."

She tried it another way, bringing it over one shoulder and across like a sari, leaving an arm and a shoulder bare. This she considered slightly better, and she glanced at Shayne's face to verify it. She still didn't like what she saw there.

"Mr. Shayne," she said, trying to sound younger, "if you knew what I went through before I said I would—"

Shayne made a slight gesture with the coiled whip. "Answer my questions. Is Jake's last name Fitch?"

She nodded.

"What does he do for a living?"

"Different things. Right now he tends bar."

"Who paid him for setting this up?"

"You know—those people. Some snooty girl."

"Candida Morse?"

"That's her name. One of those very snooty blondes."

"How much are you getting?"

"Jake said a grand. I think more. I'll find out, don't worry."

"Do you know anything about a report on a paint called 'T-239'?"

She shook her head. He slapped her again, using the

whip handle and the coiled whip but not hitting her really hard. She fell on the bed, her hand to her face.

"I never heard anybody mention it, even! Mr. Shayne, I'm a junior in high school! I'll tell you how much I got out of this so far—a couple of hundred skins. What paint? Jake never tells me why, he just says do it."

"Do you know anybody named Hallam?"

She shook her head.

"Walter Langhorne?"

"No."

"Who's Josie?"

"My guy! I mean, on top of Jake. He pays the rent for this place. We come here every Wednesday night when his wife plays bridge with her mother. He's kind of cute, really. Jake took a couple of shots of us, you know—"

A key turned in the lock. Shayne and the girl looked into each other's eyes, feeling a common emotion at last. The detective whirled. When the door opened, he was standing behind it, his cast part of the way out of the sling, ready to pivot. There would be two of them, and he didn't really think he could take care of them both.

The door closed. Shayne's swing was already underway. He checked it by catching the cast with his right arm. It wasn't Vince Camilli, the vice cop. It was Jose Despard.

His tailoring was impeccable, as usual. He had a bedside table in one hand, a small lamp in the other.

"Deedee!" he said, pleased. "You're here! What a perfectly delightful—"

Shayne's figure caught the tail of his eye, and he was given a different kind of surprise as he swung around. "Shayne!"

That was all Shayne let him say. He knocked the door out of his grasp and threw the bolt. When the raid began, he and the girl had to be somewhere else. He jerked Despard around with the hook. "Do what I tell you. We're going to have cops in a minute."

"Cops!"

Despard made an involuntary movement toward the door.

"They're between you and the elevator," Shayne snapped.

"They'll want to know who signed the lease. Tell them. Don't say anything else. Pull some rank. Don't choke up and you'll be O.K."

He snatched up the long whip he had dropped when the door opened.

"A whip!" Despard exclaimed. "Shayne, I want an explanation."

"A black Buick parked on Sycamore Lane," Shayne said. "Across the canal. Drive off in your own car and come back. I'll meet you there." He waved the whip at the girl, as though giving directions to a lion who knew no other language. "O.K., Deedee."

The girl was frozen on the bed. Shayne stuck the coiled whip in his sling, took her by the back of the neck and marched her to the terrace. Her improvised garment came apart as she moved and Despard saw the streak of fresh blood across her thighs.

"You've been whipping her! You think you can get away with this?"

He rushed the detective, who met him with an upward movement of the loaded cast. The hidden knuckles clunked against the side of his jaw and he went down.

Shayne kept his hard grip on the girl's neck. She was whimpering. They were outside on the terrace by the time he heard the first noises at the door.

One long continuous terrace had been cast for each floor. It had then been partitioned by light metal panels, providing a separate terrace for each tiny apartment. Shayne had hoped to swing around the partition to an adjoining apartment, reaching the elevator or the fire stairs while the cops were occupied in 9-C. But lights were on in the apartments on either side. He looked over the rail. The apartment directly beneath them was dark.

He thrust the girl against the railing. Without hesitation he uncoiled the whip and ran it around one of the concrete uprights, pulling the shank through the loop on the handle. When Deedee saw what he meant to do, she tried to pull away.

"You can't make me."

"Grab me around the neck and hang on, unless you want me to throw you over."

"You wouldn't!"

Shayne grinned at her.

"Oh, God," she said in a trembling voice. "I just can't."

He swung over the flat balustrade. A quick jerk of the head commanded her to follow. She was making frightened noises. Shayne tangled the hook in her long hair and yanked her toward him. She seized his neck with both thin arms. Her legs fastened themselves compulsively around his waist.

He was already letting himself down, the thin end of the whip looped around his fist. With a splintering crash, the door in the apartment sprang open as Shayne's lithe, rangy body disappeared below the balustrade. He crooked his right arm around the concrete upright, putting no weight on the whip. His feet probed out blindly. The ceilings were as low as the builder had been able to make them, and Shayne figured on a drop of no more than six feet to the railing.

The girl had a stranglehold on him. Her bare knees scraped against the rough concrete as he let himself down another few inches, still not entrusting their combined weight to the whip.

He shifted his hold. For one instant before his toes touched the concrete railing, only the stretched leather thong kept them from dropping eight floors to the embankment along the edge of the bay.

Then he was balancing lightly on the railing, his cast pressed against the terrace ceiling. He revolved so the girl was over the terrace and pried her fingers loose from his neck. He jerked at the whip handle. As soon as it came free, he threw it straight out and, without waiting to see it fall, jumped down to the girl's side.

The mattress cover had dropped at her feet. She was shuddering, her face in her hands. Shayne threw the mattress cover around her shoulders and pulled her to the door.

She started to speak, but he stopped her with a harsh

whisper. Inside, he saw the looming shapes of furniture and banged his shin painfully on a low table. There was a faint hissing sound in the room. Discerning the oval outline of a lampshade, he let go of her hand and felt for the switch.

Another light came on before he could find it. This was a tiny tensor lamp beside the bed, with a concentrated beam. The beam found Shayne.

A woman's voice said, "Stand still."

Enough light leaked out of the intense beam to show Shayne something else—a Colt .45 automatic. He said easily, "Let me turn on this other lamp. Then you can hold the gun with both hands."

His hand continued its slow movement toward the lamp. When she didn't tell him to stop, he snapped the switch, flooding the room with rosy light. This apartment was a duplicate of the one overhead in shape and size, but it contained enough furniture to crowd a much larger place. The woman in bed was wearing a cold-cream disguise and her head was a mass of exploding curlers.

She said with surprise, "You're the man with the broken arm in the elevator."

The hissing, Shayne saw, came from a vaporizer on the table by the bed.

"That's what fooled me. You went to bed with a cold."

"Don't try to change the subject," she said in a determined nasal voice, and gestured with the .45. The muzzle hole was pointed squarely at Shayne's chest, and she was squeezing the grip so hard with both hands that he knew the handle safety wouldn't be operating.

She risked a sideward glance at Deedee and exclaimed, "Why, you're as naked as a jaybird under that thing!"

The barrel of the .45 twitched back at Shayne and held steady. "Mister, you just go on holding still while I call the police. If you've got an explanation, I don't want to hear it."

Shayne started to speak and she repeated, "I don't want to hear it!"

He said in a conversational tone, "If you squeeze any harder, it's going to go off. I'm standing still. I intend to go on standing still. Call the cops, by all means. But listen to me a minute first. My name's Michael Shayne."

"No, it's not."

"I'll show you my license if you'll let me take it out."

"I'm not as foolish as I look. Hold still, you!" she said as Deedee started to move. She pawed out blindly for the phone, upsetting the vaporizer. "I'll tell you why I know you're not Michael Shayne. I saw Shayne on TV about one minute after I rode up with you in the elevator. So much for that story."

"That was a tape," Shayne said. "They taped it this afternoon. The phone's just back of your hand. Yeah, right there. Did the Mike Shayne you saw on TV have one arm in a sling?"

"Yes-s," she admitted. "It was quite a coincidence, I thought."

"Don't dial for a minute," Shayne said as she put the phone on her lap. "I traded that TV interview for some information. I've been looking for a missing girl, and here she is." He pulled the mattress cover aside to reveal the long whip mark across Deedee's thighs. "They've been keeping her upstairs in 9-C, and they locked up her clothes so she couldn't run away. They showed up at the door before I could get her out. We came down like Batman, which I don't ever want to have to do again. I'd like to show you the license."

After a moment, she said reluctantly, "Move your hand a half inch at a time."

He turned slowly and unbuttoned his hip pocket. Removing the little leather folder, he flicked it open and extended it across the foot of the bed.

"Not so close," she said. "I'm farsighted."

He pulled it back slowly until she nodded. He put it away and she aimed the gun somewhere else, to Shayne's relief.

"I guess that's who you are, then. Who's she?"

"I haven't found out her name yet. You've heard about white slavery?"

"Oh, yes—sure. Is she one?"

Shayne nodded gravely.

The woman put the gun aside and pulled back the covers. "Still and all, regardless of how she makes a living, we don't want her to run around town in her birthday suit, do we?"

She picked a dressing gown off the back of the nearest chair, then changed her mind and went to the closet, from which she took a much tackier garment of dark blue terry-cloth.

"Never mind returning it unless you want to, Mr. Shayne. It's outlived its usefulness. And I don't want my name to appear publicly in this in any way."

Shayne assured her she could count on his discretion. Deedee shrugged into the robe, which was several sizes too large.

"Maybe I can find a pair of slippers you could put on, honey," the lady said.

"She's all right barefoot," Shayne told her.

"I'll look out and see if the coast is clear, anyway," the lady offered, going to the door. "I could even go down in the elevator with you, if you can wait till I take out the curlers."

"We'll be all right now," Shayne said. "Which way to the stairs?"

She pointed. After they went out she stood in the doorway watching them. Then, with a deep sigh, she turned back into her crowded apartment. The door swung shut behind her.

CHAPTER 10

"And just what is white slavery, may I ask?" Deedee said haughtily on the fire stairs. "If it's what I think it is—"

Shayne grinned. "Ask your parents."

"That's a laugh. First I'd have to find them. What are you going to do with me?"

"What do you think I ought to do?"

She looked at him suspiciously, to see if he was serious. "Why, let me go, as soon as I answer the rest of your questions. I'm going to cooperate a hundred percent. You don't want to have me arrested. All that red tape, Mr. Shayne, I know how busy you are—"

She trailed off when he failed to reply. Several more times on the way down she tried to continue the subject, but the grim set of his mouth discouraged her. Between the fourth floor and the third, she began to feel dizzy and told him she had to stop and sit down. He ignored her. She pulled his arm in hard against her breast.

"I'm about ready to flop! Honestly and truly. I don't get enough exercise."

Shayne still didn't slow down.

They passed the first floor and continued to the basement. She went on revolving even after Shayne had stopped, reeling back in to clutch him with both hands, the robe flying. He put her aside, opened the door and looked out carefully.

The cinderblock corridor was dimly lit by forty-watt bulbs. Hearing footsteps, Shayne let the door swing nearly shut as a man in work clothes, carrying a mop and a pail, came out of the elevator, left mop and pail in a storage closet and entered another room. Through the open door, Shayne could hear TV voices, the sound of screeching tires, then gunfire. A baby was crying.

He pulled Deedee into the corridor and motioned to her to open a door. She did so. He felt for the light switch and turned it on. It was a storeroom, jammed with bikes, baby carriages, cots and luggage, with three windows high in the back wall.

"What was Jake going to do?" he asked. "Wait to see what happened?"

"Uh-huh. In case you didn't show up, he'd have to lay a few bills on the cops, to keep everybody happy."

"Where is he?"

"I guess in his car."

Shayne snapped his fingers twice and she said hastily, "A new air-conditioned DeSoto, and it's double-parked at the dead end if he didn't move it. I'll show you exactly where. Believe me, Mr. Shayne, I'm cooperating right down the line."

He put out his hand. "Let's have the robe."

She pulled it together defensively. "I won't try to get away. I won't budge an inch."

He continued to hold out his hand. She made a pleading face, but her sense of realism won. "Aah!" She shrugged out of the robe and gave it to him.

"Maybe I'll walk out of here like this and get a taxi."

"They're scarce around here," he said.

He looked into the corridor. The door of the superintendent's apartment was still open. He hesitated. He didn't want any trouble while the raiding party was still in the building.

"O.K., I'm going out the window. When I get out, turn off the light."

"And what if somebody comes in for a baby buggy or something?"

"Hold still. They'll think you're a statue."

He kicked a trunk into position beneath one of the windows and pulled out the screen. Pushing his cast ahead of him, he pulled himself up and out. The light winked off behind him.

He went around the building. Protected by a screen of low-growing shrubs, he spotted the DeSoto where Deedee had said it would be parked. There was a figure at the wheel.

After a moment's reflection, Shayne returned to the back of the building and stepped down off the embankment onto the strip of hard sand at the water's edge. He walked on to the canal, came back up on the embankment and approached the DeSoto from behind.

He pulled open the door on the passenger's side and slid into the cool interior. The man at the wheel swung around.

Shayne left the door open slightly so the dome light would stay on and they could look at each other. Jake Fitch was swarthy and unshaven, with bushy eyebrows which almost met over a meaty nose. His forearms were hairy, and heavy black hair tufted out of the neck of his shirt, his ears, his nostrils. He was wearing a blue linen cap with some kind of insignia.

His eyes flickered at Shayne's cast and his hand shot toward the glove compartment. Shayne raised the cast and waited. Jake touched the glove compartment button, the little door fell open, and Shayne moved the cast forward and upward, slapping him on the temple with the brass knuckles.

He sat back, stunned. Shayne felt inside the glove compartment and brought out a Walther .38, one of the prettiest of the European handguns.

Jake mumbled something while the detective lit a cigarette.

"Take your time," Shayne said. "I'm in no hurry."

He smoked in silence. Jake recovered gradually. He was functioning again by the time Shayne finished his cigarette and stubbed it out against his heel.

Jake touched his forehead and looked for blood on his fingers. "What did you have to do that for? I didn't do anything."

"I can't really believe that," Shayne remarked.

Working the slide of the little Belgian automatic with one hand, he checked to be sure it was loaded. Then he brought it around in the flat of his right hand and slapped Jake with it.

Jake yelped. He came down hard on the door handle and hurled himself sideward. Shayne raked out with the hook, which snagged in Jake's pants. Jake didn't understand what was holding him, and he went on trying to get away. The hook ripped through his pants and buried itself in the soft flesh of his thigh.

"Close the door," Shayne said coldly. "I'm feeling less good-natured every minute."

Jake eased back in, going with the pull. As he came all the way in the light went off. He put both hands on Shayne's cast and tried to work it toward him. Shayne dropped his elbow and the hook dug in deeper.

"Please," Jake begged. "Shayne, don't—that's—they

weren't supposed to do anything to you last night but tap you a couple. When I get hold of that Whitey, I'll break him in two."

"What about this setup with Deedee?"

Jake's weight shifted back against the door and the light blinked on. There was a look of intense alarm on his face.

"Shayne, what are you, anyway?" he cried frantically. "How did you find out about that?" The light went off. "It's not how it looks! Give me a break! Don't pull so hard. It wasn't a real frame. We didn't play it to stick. She just wanted us to keep you wrapped up a few days."

"Who?"

"Miss Morse! Miss Morse! Take the hook out, *will you, please?* Any questions, I'll be happy to answer them."

"Whose idea was the whip?"

"Hers. She mapped out the whole goddamn thing, the whip, the dialogue. I don't claim to be any great brain."

"How long have you worked for her?"

"Off and on. One year, two years."

"Fifty thousand bucks," Shayne said. "April twenty-third."

"How would I know?" Jake demanded. "She wrote it down for Deedee to say on the phone. We figured it for a come-on, to make sure you showed up. Like that crack about murder. Who's been murdered? What fifty thousand? The kind of dough I've been seeing is a hell of a lot less than fifty, believe me."

"April twenty-third," Shayne repeated. "Think about it."

"I did think about it! I thought about it all afternoon. I planted Deedee on Jose Despard along around the first of April. If anything happened the twenty-third, I don't know what. That's six months back! The kind of memory I've got, I'm lucky if I remember last week."

"When you planted Dedee how?"

"Well, I found out he likes them that age, so I asked at her high school if anybody might be interested. He thought he raped her—she's only supposed to be fourteen. Shayne, I'm bleeding like a pig, you know that? You want me to bleed to death?"

"It can't be that bad yet," Shayne said. "How soon did you take the pictures?"

"Right away, right away. On the first night, when he thought he raped her. I'm no photographer, but they come out great. I thought it was strictly a one-shot, but when I turn over the pix, they tell me to string him along, Despard."

"That brings us back to the twenty-third of April."

"I'm telling you! Miss Morse pulled a date out of the hat, to make it sound better. Be human, can't you, Shayne? With that hook in my leg, don't you think I'd tell you if I remembered? There's a main artery in there somewhere."

Shayne opened the door to turn on the light again. Jake was sweating in the chilly air. His mouth twitched as Shayne looked at the spot where the hook went into his leg.

"I think I missed it by about a quarter of an inch," Shayne said. "Don't make me nervous. My hands shake when people lie to me."

Jake clapped both hands on top of Shayne's cast to hold it steady. "I'm not lying! I'm down at the bottom of this operation. 'Why' is a question I never ask. All I ask is 'How?' and 'How much does the job pay?' If I started asking 'Why,' they'd get themselves somebody with a smaller mouth. Take for example, did Hal Begley or Miss Morse tell me why they wanted you jammed up with Deedee? Like hell they told me."

"I see we'll have to sit here a while longer," Shayne said. "I'm going to light another cigarette. Try not to move."

He shook a cigarette out of the package and lit it with the dashboard lighter. The hook changed position slightly and grated against bone. Jake whimpered.

"Don't tell them I told you," he said hopelessly. "Those Begleys, I don't like to be in the same town with them and be on bad terms. But I'm flesh and blood. They got me the job at the club, like the middle of April."

"What club?"

"North Miami Country, tending bar. And they give me a list of names. They want me behind the stick so I can make book on certain members. In that location I know who's in the club, when they come in, when they go out."

"Was Despard on the list?"

"Sure. The whole bunch from that company. Langhorne —he's on the board of governors. Hallam, Jr. The whole outfit. Jackson, Hill, Ringley. Christ, I don't know—eight, nine. I still got the list at home. When one of those certain characters came in, I was supposed to mark it down. When he went out, mark it down."

"For how long?"

"A week, ten days."

"All you did was clock eight or nine people in and out?" Shayne said thoughtfully.

"That's all," Jake said without hesitation.

The promptness of the reply told Shayne there was more to come. He continued to smoke. Jake glanced at him quickly, and glanced away. He stood it for one more moment, then burst out, "I had to check a certain locker!"

"Yeah," Shayne said. "Whose?"

"An empty locker, it wasn't rented to anybody. Miss Morse gave me the number and combination. When nobody was using the locker room, I ducked in and looked to see if a package was in that locker, and wrote down the time."

"That's fine," Shayne said with no change of expression. "And one day there was a package."

"Yeah."

"Did you take it out or leave it?"

"I left it. They wouldn't trust me with anything high level—I told you. I notified her."

"Is Begley a member of the club?"

"He has a card. The next day, same thing. I kept checking the locker. No package. A while later, package. A while after that, no package again. I wrote it down."

"Now get set for the big question," Shayne said.

"Don't ask me," Jake said earnestly. "I don't know the answer! But I know what you're trying to establish—I didn't just get in from the boondocks, after all. I know they're in the spy business, and somebody from Despard's put a package in the locker. Begley picked it up. Begley put a package of money in and somebody picked that up. But I don't know who! They were coming and going all the time, both days. Oh, I ruled out a couple. Hill and Jackson I crossed off in my own mind, they weren't in the club either day. I could make up a name for you and get off the hook, but what good would it do? Off the hook," he said sardonically, "funny joke, Fitch. When you found out I was faking, you'd come looking for me, and to face facts, I think you'd probably find me."

"Why did you stay at the club afterward?"

"It's a job. She didn't want me to quit right away, so it wouldn't look suspicious. That's the whole bit, Shayne. Now the next thing we want to do is get this leg to a doctor's, don't we?"

He made a small sound, and Shayne turned to follow his look, letting the overhead light blink off.

Two men approached. Shayne recognized one of them. It was the vice-squad detective named Vince Camilli. He was tieless, but he wore a jacket over his gun, which he used far too often. He had a handsome dark face, a loose mouth. He was the department's top scorer in both homosexual and prostitution arrests, and Shayne was sure that the total included many entrapment cases using fabricated evidence, as well as shakedowns that had failed to pay off.

Camilli spoke to his partner, a weedy young man in a sports shirt, who was trying to raise a mustache. Shayne pulled the end of the sling down over the buried hook.

The younger cop held back while Camilli came up to the driver's side of the DeSoto and made a cranking gesture. Jake rolled down the window.

"Something wrong, Camilli?" he said nervously.

The detective reached in with his left hand, on which he wore a rough signet ring, and ground the ring against Jake's face.

"Next time check it out first, will you? We looked like a couple of bums in there."

"You had the right apartment, nine C?"

"We had the right apartment. What do you think this is, Fitch, amateur night?"

"I just got this tip, that's all. I passed it on the way I heard it."

"The apartment's rented to the vice-president of a manufacturing firm. His credentials are perfectly O.K."

Jake had his hand on the door. Without haste, Camilli pulled out his police special and slammed it down on the other's fingers. Jake snatched his hand back inside the car with a cry.

"A couple of people have won suits for false arrest lately," Camilli went on, "and this town is full of lawyers."

He pulled the door open enough to trip the dome switch, and looked in. "Mike Shayne," he said, surprised. "Well, well, Mr. Bill of Rights in person, the guy who thinks queers and floozies are covered by the United States Constitution."

"Back to work, Camilli," Shayne said. "There are hustlers out all over town and here you are taking things easy."

Camilli scowled. "This begins to make sense. You think I can't smell a frame when I stick my nose in it? Let me tell you something. I'm making a mental note, Shayne. The next time you want somebody taken care of, let me handle it for you. But bring me in on the planning, will you? Don't spring it on me, just to get out of it cheap."

"You're through here, aren't you, Camilli?"

"For the time being. I said to myself when I watched that performance of yours on TV tonight, I said to myself, what do you know? Shayne has been reached. Not that I expect you to tell me the ins and outs, because I'm only a poor, lowly copper."

He straightened, then stooped again to give Shayne a hard look. Shayne returned it. Camilli picked up his partner and they walked off together.

"Now?" Jake said anxiously.

"Let's have your wallet."

Jake's mouth twitched a protest, but he produced his wallet after a reminder from the buried hook. Shayne flipped it open and thumbed the bills out on his lap.

"Leave me twenty," Jake begged. "I'll need it to pay the doctor."

Shayne flicked two tens back at him and fanned the rest. "Call it three-fifty even," he said. "I'll give you a receipt. It's probably not enough to keep you in town, but it may help."

"Why wouldn't I stay in town?"

Shayne pulled an envelope out of the glove compartment and scribbled an IOU. Then he wrenched the hook out of Jake's leg. Reaching over to the floor of the back seat, he gathered up Deedee's clothing.

"Shayne, it's coming in spurts!"

Shayne pushed the door open on his side. "No, it's not. Get them to show you a chart at the hospital. The artery's on the other side of the leg. Here." He sorted out the girl's underclothing, keeping only her dress and a pair of shoes. "Bandage yourself with this. If you think you need a tourniquet, use the bra."

He got out and slammed the door, leaving Jake whimpering for help inside. Before Shayne reached the entrance to the apartment building, the DeSoto went by him, already going very fast.

CHAPTER 11

The light was on in the basement room where Shayne had left the girl. She had opened a trunk to look for something to wear, so far without success. She whirled, protecting her breasts. Seeing Shayne, she dropped her arms and came toward him.

"Hey, my dress. Did you see Jake?"

"Yeah. He was very disappointed to hear you didn't do better upstairs."

He tossed her the dress. She looked to see if he had

anything else for her to wear underneath, then pulled it over her head and wriggled into it.

"I don't see how he can blame me," she said. "You didn't give me one minute to think."

He handed her a shoe at a time, and she hopped from foot to foot putting them on. She smoothed the dress over her hips.

"Big improvement," she commented sarcastically. "You can see right through it. I hope we're not going anyplace in public."

"What's your real name?"

"Deedee's my real name. I had to put up a terrific battle, but everybody calls me by it, finally." She added, "My *real* name is Dorothy Pappas. Do I look like a Dorothy Pappas?"

"Where's your family live?"

"What family? They booted me out when I thought I was preg."

He jerked his head. They went down the corridor to the elevator, passing the superintendent's door. The super and his wife were watching television and they didn't look around.

In the elevator Deedee stood very close to Shayne, her breasts touching his arm.

"I guess you don't like me much."

"Not a hell of a lot," Shayne told her.

"I didn't guess so."

Outside, he strode rapidly toward the spot where he had left his car. She clicked beside him, not quite keeping up. Jose Despard was waiting on the sidewalk beside Shayne's Buick, his shoulders hunched, both hands deep in his pockets. He gulped when he saw the girl.

She ran the last few steps, one hand out, but stopped before she actually touched him. "Honey, I'm so sorry it had to happen! As sorry as I can be. You know you weren't supposed to be in on it."

His face contorted painfully. At a brusque signal from Shayne, she got in the Buick.

"Wait here for me," Shayne told Despard.

Despard kept his head averted. While Shayne went

through the pattern involved in starting the car with one hand, Despard said in a choked voice, "Don't forget to put something on that cut."

"On my legs?" she said. "No, I'll take care of it. I won't see you again, will I, so—well, goodbye."

Despard didn't trust himself to answer.

Shayne turned onto Biscayne Boulevard, then pulled over to use the phone. On the third try he found a friend who said she would be willing to put Deedee up for the night.

"Man or woman?" Deedee said when they were moving again.

"Woman."

"And she's probably just a bit dykey, huh," Deedee said sullenly after another moment.

Shayne glanced at her and she said with spirit, "Don't look at *me*. I happen to be heterosexual and proud of it."

"You happen to be what?"

"Heterosexual. That means—"

"I know what it means."

He delivered her to a Northwest address, promising to explain in the morning how he found himself the custodian of a high-school dropout wearing no underwear. He returned to the Buena Vista street corner. Despard, told by Shayne to stay put, hadn't moved. He had pulled himself together to the extent of being able to fill and light a pipe. Shayne motioned him to the driver's side.

"You drive," he said. "First, hand me the phone book."

Despard reached all the way over to the shelf behind the back seat. The detective looked up the address listed for Candida Morse.

"Coral Gables. Avenue Muleta. Go over to North Miami Avenue and pick up the Expressway."

After knocking out his pipe, Despard made a U-turn to join the traffic on 4th Avenue. His narrow, balding head nodded and bobbed at the end of a stalklike neck. He was trying not to look at Shayne, but his head kept turning.

"What do I do, thank you?" he said bitterly. "Or didn't you arrange that? What kind of a hold do you have over her?"

"I won't try to figure out what you're talking about," Shayne said. "The cops probably gave you a rough time before they found out who you were. You happened to walk in at the wrong time, that's all. But I doubt if you'll have any more Wednesday-evening dates with the girl. Something's missing there, Despard. Some vital little connection, and who's responsible for it is none of my business, or yours either. If she had all the usual parts, she'd go out with teenage boys and be interested in whatever the hell teenagers are interested in nowadays. But then she wouldn't have been interested in seducing you, would she?"

"I'm the one who did the seducing," Despard said miserably.

"That's what they wanted you to think," Shayne said. "She was planted on you by Hal Begley Associates, working through a small-time crumb named Jake Fitch."

"Jake Fitch!" The pale face bobbed around again. "You don't know what you're talking about. He's her father."

"They may be living together. He's not her father."

For an instant Shayne thought Despard would lose control of the wheel. The Buick drifted across the line, narrowly missing an oncoming car. Sawing at the wheel, Despard brought it back. His Adam's apple was working.

"I don't suppose you'd say that so positively unless you know it for a fact. Something terrible must have happened to her when she was young. I thought—"

"You were wrong," Shayne said briefly. "How did she get you alone?"

"She was sent by the baby-sitting agency. I drove her home. Her father was still working. Jake Fitch was still working. Fitch," he repeated, pronouncing the name with revulsion. "Her *lover?* I shared her with Jake Fitch?"

"Move it along, will you, Despard?"

"She was afraid to go in alone. She thought she saw a shadow moving on an upstairs shade. She made me go up to make sure no one was there." He swallowed heavily. "If that was acting, she did a good job."

"I doubt if she had to carry you upstairs," Shayne said dryly. "How much have they taken you for?"

"Not a cent! Oh, I've given her presents, perfume, a new dress. I leased the apartment. But my wife happens to run the checkbook in my house, and I assure you I couldn't sneak any sizeable sum past her."

"If that checks out," Shayne said, "I'll have to report I've located the man who sold the T-239 folder."

The Buick slowed abruptly. "Shayne, you have to be joking. Damn it, I can't talk and drive at the same time."

They were on 43rd Street, between First Avenue and North Miami. At a signal from Shayne, Despard pulled over to the curb. Turning all the way around, he said passionately, using both hands, "I didn't do it. I don't care what kind of blackmail they tried to use on me, I wouldn't—"

"What are the photographs like?"

"Photographs? You mean they have pictures of me? *Of me and Deedee?"* He covered his face. "My God."

"They were taken the first night," Shayne said. "Jake said they turned out well. What would your wife do if they showed up in the mail some morning?"

"God," Despard said again.

"How old do you think the girl is?"

Despard raised his head slowly. "I don't think. I know. I happened to see a form she was making out. She's fourteen. But she's mature for her age."

"She's seventeen," Shayne said. "The form was a fake. The point of this whole operation was to make you think they could break up your family, get you canned from your clubs and slam you in jail for that fine old felony known as statutory rape. Not many people have a stiff enough spine to hold out against that kind of a parlay. Fitch is working for a blackmail and extortion outfit. You can't tell me they had that kind of ammunition without intending to use it."

Despard lifted both trembling hands. He worked his Adam's apple for a moment before he could bring out any words.

"It's—it's absolutely the first time I've had the slightest hint of any such suggestion. I'll repeat that under oath."

"You may have to."

Despard dropped one hand to Shayne's shoulder. "You must believe me."

"Take your hand off me," Shayne said.

Despard pulled it back as though burned. "I see how you feel. I'm the lowest of the low. I have this—tendency. I love youthfulness. I don't like to feel old. But with Deedee it was the first time I ever—continued where I wasn't wanted. She fought like a cat. And now you tell me it wasn't real." His eyes contracted. "Yes, there were signs. There were definite signs. A certain—lubricity. I thought afterward I was trying to fool myself, but perhaps—yes, if her resistance had been genuine, perhaps I would have stopped." He seemed relieved.

"Let's hope so," Shayne said. "Do you play much golf at the North Miami Country Club?"

"Why, yes," Despard said, the change of subject sending his eyebrows up. "I get in a couple of rounds every weekend, and I usually manage one or two during the week. Why?"

"That's where Begley picked up the report."

"I had nothing to do with it," Despard said firmly. "I had access to it, I won't deny that. My secretary has a Thermofax machine, not that I know how to work it. I played a lot of golf last spring, trying to overcome a slice. But don't stop looking for the person who really did it, because I didn't." He looked ahead through the windshield, holding himself erect. "It's old-fashioned, but I like to think I believe in honor."

Shayne made a rude sound.

Despard said stiffly, "You're entitled to that response. I make this distinction. Despards have often been in various kinds of trouble. We have lost too much money at the gambling tables. We have fought duels. We have committed adultery, and had sexual relations with unmarried girls. But we have not, Shayne, we have never betrayed the honor of our family, our country or the company we work for."

"I suppose Despards were officers in the Confederate Army."

"We ended as officers. We began as recruits. My great-great-grandfather rose to command a division of cavalry."

Shayne lit a cigarette deliberately. "Where does Hallam stand on the Civil War?"

"Nowhere," Despard said, still very stiff. "He is a part of a different tradition. All we could discover when he married my sister was the name of one maternal grandparent, a New Englander, who ended his life as a clerk in a cotton house."

"And you've probably rubbed that in often enough so he'd enjoy hearing about this trouble with Deedee?"

Despard bit off the words. "He might. Are you going to tell him?"

"No, not yet. There's more involved here than the theft of a paint formula. I don't want to commit myself before I know a little more."

"What do you mean, more involved?"

"I can go into the next board-of-directors meeting with the facts I have and nail you to the wall. You know that. They'll ask for your resignation on a dozen counts. And that will put Hallam in complete control. Or am I wrong?"

"You surely don't mean *Hallam* is behind this?"

"I don't know a damn thing except what people have been telling me," the detective said sharply. "I don't think he had anything to do with setting up Deedee. But after you fell for that, it's possible he found out about it and brought me in to get confirmation so it wouldn't seem there was any personal malice involved. When I say it's possible, I don't mean it's likely. I've managed to stay alive this long by playing the odds. You're the odds-on favorite on the morning line, Despard. But I don't have to put my money down till Hallam gets back from Washington. If honor kept you from turning over that report, there's somebody else in the company who's either not so honorable or more pressed. I'll give you twelve hours to see if you can come up with anything."

"Twelve hours! What can I do in twelve hours? You can't believe I'll suddenly be thinking about it for the first time!"

Shayne made an impatient gesture. "Now you've got an incentive. I've already been paid two thousand. All I have to do to collect the eight-thousand-dollar balance is turn in a thief. You'll do. If you don't want to be turned in, give me somebody else."

"I'm not an informer," Despard said with another attempt at dignity.

"In that case you're dead," Shayne told him. "Oh, they'll give you five minutes to defend yourself, and you can make your speech. I don't think they'll believe you. I happen to believe you myself, but that's partly because I don't think you've had your chance yet to find out how you'd stand up under real pressure."

Despard looked at him suspiciously. "I had the impression you thought I was lying."

"There was money involved," Shayne explained. "They picked up the report one day and paid for it the next. They could get it from you for nothing. Not only that. I don't think you would have gone on having sex with Deedee after you saw the photographs."

Despard shuddered. "I'm not in my dotage yet."

"Another point. This Candida Morse is a bright girl. Too bright to think she could hurt me with this kind of vice-cop frame-up. It's too crude and too obvious. I think the real reason for that was to lower my opinion of her intelligence, so I'd jump at the name Despard when I heard it. Deedee had been told to make sure I heard it, obviously to fake me away from their real contact."

"I agree with you," Despard said ironically. "I didn't do it. That's what I've been telling you."

"They had a limited time to come up with the report," Shayne continued. "If they couldn't produce it in a month or maybe a month and a half, the deal would peter out. So they wouldn't want to bet their whole bankroll on a single entry. They hired Fitch and Deedee to work on you. Candida went after Walter Langhorne herself on a recruitment basis, and maybe that was the one that worked. Statutory rape is tricky and dangerous, and they wouldn't use it unless they had to. And maybe they were working on a third possibility. Probably three was all they had time for. All right. All these arguments weigh with me, but unless you can produce some hard information for me tonight or tomorrow morning, I won't even put them in the report. I've been looking for a handle. Now that I have one, you'd better believe I mean to use it. As soon as you have something to tell me, call me on the car phone. If that doesn't answer, try Tim Rourke."

"I'm no detective. I don't even know how to begin."

"Begin by thinking about it," Shayne said. "Who needed money? Who was in trouble? Who had more money and was in less trouble on April twenty-fourth than on April twenty-third? Get to work, Despard. You haven't much time."

CHAPTER 12

At first Shayne thought the phone-book address was a misprint. Then he saw a narrow cobbled lane leading between two stucco houses built in the fake-Moorish style of the mid-1920s, ending in a paved court.

He tried Candida's number again and again got no answer. He left the Buick in a University of Miami parking lot and entered the court on foot. The house he was looking for was a low building which seemed to be a remodeled stable, in spite of the fact that Coral Gables had been built after city people stopped keeping horses. The building contained three duplex apartments. The one in the middle, with "Candida Morse" in decorative script over the wrought-iron bell pull, was dark.

Shayne snapped his lighter to look at the lock. The lock itself presented no problem, but the massive half-inch bolt could only be forced with heavier equipment than Shayne carried with him. He went around to look at the kitchen door. That, too, had been reinforced. He pushed his cast through the kitchen window, reached in carefully and unlocked it. A moment later he was inside the house.

After turning on the light, he broke the slivers of glass still clinging to the sash, found a broom and swept the mess under the kitchen table.

He searched the downstairs carefully. A small antique secretary in the living room had one locked drawer, which he forced. Inside, he found Candida's passport, her college diploma, copies of income-tax forms for earlier years, bundles of letters and canceled checks. He flipped through the passport to see how much traveling she did, and found her birthdate. She was twenty-seven. The letters were in their original envelopes. He checked the postmarks without finding anything current enough to interest him.

A steep, narrow staircase led to the second floor. In Candida's bedroom, a very feminine room which she had passed through in a hurry, changing clothes on the run, Shayne looked around speculatively, rubbing his jaw with the ball of his thumb. His reflection in a big mirror over the bureau caught his eye. He needed maintenance. His sling was torn and dirty. His shirt was black with oil and dirty cobwebs picked up crawling out of the basement window of the Buena Vista apartment house.

He continued to look around. The headboard of the oversize bed was divided into compartments holding books, a clock-radio, a phone. He pulled open a sliding drawer and gave a grunt of satisfaction, seeing three flat metal boxes, the size of a standard safe-deposit box, each tagged with a number. Shayne picked the box with the highest number. He worked on it with the flat chisel blade of a combination tool, holding the box with the weight of his cast. He twisted slowly, increasing the pressure, and the lid sprang open.

He grinned when he saw what the box contained.

He emptied it on the bureau. In an unmarked envelope there were four 35-millimeter negatives. He held one to the light. It showed a man and a girl on the floor. The girl was only partially clothed. Her blouse was torn. The man's face didn't show, but Shayne had no doubt that in an enlarged print the narrow head and thin fringe of hair would be recognized as belonging to Jose Despard.

In the same envelope was a slip of paper with a number and a padlock combination. On a separate page there was a kind of timetable, giving the arrivals and departures of seven or eight people, identified by initials, over a ten-day period. Finally, there was a small film can. Inside it was a tightly wound roll of microfilm. Shayne unrolled an inch or so. It was the top-secret T-239 report.

Still grinning happily, he transferred these objects to various pockets and put the rifled box back in the headboard compartment.

Again the disreputable figure in the mirror caught his eye. He pulled off the sling and worked the shirt over his head and then over the cast. After washing his hands and face, he made a new sling from one of Candida's pillow slips. Then he washed out the shirt, using part of a bottle of shampoo. He wrung it with one hand. While he was draping it over the shower rail he heard a door open downstairs.

He went to the hall.

"I really *do* seem to be rattled," he heard Candida's voice say. "I left all the lights on. I never do that."

There were footsteps. The door closed.

A man's voice said, "Let's take a trip, shall we, after we get the check? I need a vacation. I'm so damn tense it isn't funny."

"Hal, darling, you're worrying about Michael Shayne again, and will you please stop? I have that situation in hand. Jake Fitch will be calling me promptly at nine. It won't be with bad news."

"I need a drink."

Shayne called down, "So do I. Make one for me."

He returned to the bedroom and finished brushing his

hair. Then he went down the cramped stairs, ducking his head to keep from hitting the low ceiling.

Candida and her employer were standing in the hall below. They watched him emerge—his legs, his fresh sling, then his powerful bare torso. Candida was wearing a straight skirt and a sleeveless evening sweater, buttoned down the front. She had partly turned toward the living room, and Shayne saw that the sweater had no back whatever. Begley's clothes were a little too sharp, as always. The weekend of heavy drinking had taken the highlights out of his tan.

He said thickly, "This is what you mean when you say you have Shayne in hand? You absolutely don't give a damn who you get into bed with, do you?"

"Don't be childish," she said with her usual coolness.

"Who's being childish?" Begley shouted, turning on her. "Me? I'm being childish? That's your opinion?"

"Be quiet, Hal. He obviously broke in and he's just leaving. I don't know why he's not wearing a shirt."

"I had to wash it," Shayne said. "I've been crawling out windows. If you don't have cognac, I'll take bourbon."

"You didn't invite him?" Begley said. "You haven't hit the sack with him yet? Now there's a switch."

He came around to face Shayne, nervously unbuttoning his jacket. He was an inch or two over six feet, broad and solid through the chest. At one time he might have been able to stand up to the detective, but he had spent too much time lately making money.

"Miss Morse wants you to leave," he said. "Leave. We'll mail you the shirt. Don't think you've got any immunity because of that broken arm. Under your own steam or otherwise, take your pick."

Shayne stepped in close, his right arm at his side. Begley held his eyes, waiting for the right to the body. Shayne half-feinted with his right shoulder, then struck with the cast.

The hook caught the expensive fabric of Begley's light sports jacket and tore downward, taking part of his shirt and possibly some flesh with it. Begley flailed out without waiting to get set. Shayne yanked him off balance and blocked the blow easily. Then, his lips twisting, he brought the cast up hard.

The hook tore loose. Begley took two wandering steps backward, collided with an upholstered chair and sat down. Candida hurried to him.

"At this point," Shayne said, "you offer to settle."

"Wha—?" Begley said.

Candida turned with a flare of her skirt. "The devil we'll settle! We have nothing to talk to you about, so now that you've asserted yourself on your usual level, why don't you go upstairs and get your wet shirt and get the hell out of here?"

Her voice was shaking. He grinned at her.

"He owns the firm. Let's give him a chance to make up his own mind."

Begley felt his jaw and finally managed to close it. "Settle?" he said, pronouncing only one syllable. He attempted to concentrate. "How much?"

"I'm not talking about money," Shayne said. "You can't outbid Despard's. Give us the name of your contact, get United States to withhold the new paint and we won't take anybody into court."

Begley stared up, beginning to function again. After a moment he said quietly, "Is that a serious offer?"

Candida put in, "Naturally it's not serious. It's a trick."

"It may not be," Begley said slowly. "Shayne knows how hard it is to get enough evidence to impress a judge. I'd like to hear more about it. Candy, pour me a small slug of Scotch, please. I'm not up to that long walk across the room."

After glancing at Shayne, she went into the kitchen. Begley went on, his eyes narrowing, "To be realistic, you can't hope to get a cancellation at this late date. They're in too deep. They might listen to a two- or three-month postponement. That would give your people a chance to get organized. I don't say Perkins will like it, but you outweigh us financially, and if we can avoid a bruising fight—"

Candida came back. Making no comment, she handed

him a tumbler partly filled with straight whiskey. She had brought the bottle and two more glasses. She let Shayne make his own.

Begley emptied his glass without pausing for breath. He stood up, steadying himself on the back of the chair until he felt it was safe to let go.

"I don't want to say anything more before I've talked to my principal. He's in town, as it happens. Candida's been handling this account. Now that I know which way the wind is blowing, I think I'll let you talk to her about it. I'll sound out Perkins. Let Candida know where I can reach you."

"Will he take your advice?" Shayne asked.

"I imagine so. He's a reasonable sort."

He was trying hard to keep up the pretense of being a top man in a competitive business, but the cracks showed. He straightened his jacket.

"Incidentally, Shayne," he said, turning, "I'm thinking of cutting back on the more freewheeling aspects of the business. The take, frankly, is not that good. If I go back to recruitment full time, I see no reason why I should impinge on you or you should impinge on me. There's enough legitimate money lying around for both of us."

"I thought you wanted it all."

"No, just my fair share."

He went out. A moment later Shayne heard a motor start in the court. He poured himself a drink.

"He's getting ready to dump you," he said, drinking.

"Oh?" she said coldly.

"It's his one out. You had charge of the Deedee business, and he's going to maintain that the dirty work was strictly yours. If he moves fast enough, he may even get away with it."

"Very transparent, Michael. I know you'd like to drive a wedge between us. It's the oldest ruse in the world. Far from being dumped, as you put it, I'm being made a full partner."

Shayne gave her an amused look. "In return for what? For giving me Walter Langhorne?"

She gave a tired sigh. "It's true Hal and I have different views on how to proceed. It's been wearing, to say the least. I'll need a couple of anacin before I can deal with that remark. Please help yourself to the whiskey. I'll be back in a moment."

Shayne lifted his glass to her and sat down on the sofa. As soon as she was out of sight, he kicked off his shoes and followed, taking his drink.

He made no noise on the stairs, but a floorboard creaked beneath him in the upstairs hall. Candida was on the other side of the bed. She whirled, holding the empty safe-deposit box.

"Damn you!" she said. "Damn you, Mike Shayne! I thought you were a little too sure of yourself."

"Does it make that much difference? Deedee and Fitch and Despard have all been talking to me steadily for the last hour."

She threw the metal box on the bed. "I thought it would be safer here than at the office. How wrong I was! What are you going to do with it?"

"Put a few people in jail," he told her, coming into the bedroom. "Whether that includes you is going to depend on how much you tell me. I don't want to take this extortion setup to the cops. The wrong people will be hurt. In my book—and it's an argument I have with certain vice cops in this town—the crime called 'entrapment' is worse than a little extracurricular sex between a middle-aged man and a teenage girl who doesn't give much of a damn as long as there's money in it. What's Begley's idea of a solution that will satisfy everybody?"

She bit her lip without answering.

"Walter Langhorne wouldn't be bad, as a matter of fact," Shayne said. "He's in no position to complain. We might be willing to settle for Langhorne. What's your objection?"

"Because he—"

She stopped.

Shayne said, "Because he didn't do it or because you liked him?"

"I did like him. I liked him terribly."

"Spies aren't supposed to like people," Shayne commented. "It gets in the way."

She shook back her hair. "They aren't supposed to trust anybody, either, and I don't trust you, Mike Shayne. You talk about a solution that will satisfy everybody. That's pure hypocrisy, and you know it. Somebody has to win, somebody has to lose. If we let you beat us again, we're finished. Don't get Hal Begley, because all a private detective named Shayne has to do is clear his throat and they fall to pieces. Any intelligence assignments that came our way from then on would be the dangerous ones other firms had already turned down."

"What's wrong with being a simple executive recruiter?"

"It's so damn dull!" she burst out. "You ought to understand that, if anybody can. Mike, spell out the alternatives, will you?"

"I have Deedee. That's a front-page story even without Despard's name. It's libel-proof."

She nodded thoughtfully. "I used to think there was no such thing as bad publicity. Hal Begley, the Agency That Gets Results. But this, I'm afraid—"

Meeting him at the foot of the bed, she took the glass out of his hand. She shuddered after drinking from it.

"How can you drink it straight like that? Well, Mike. I've been making mistakes. Having you beaten up was a mistake. Trying to hurt you with Deedee was a mistake."

He grinned at her.

"And what's that expression supposed to mean?" she asked. "Don't you think I mean it?"

"You keep telling me things."

She looked puzzled, then shook it off. Her tongue flicked across her lips.

"Mike, it may very well be that you have too many cards in your hand. Can I have a little time or do I have to decide this minute?"

"What's going to change five minutes from now?"

"I was thinking of longer. Could I have a couple of hours?"

"Why?"

"Mike, to catch my breath! I don't know how you did it, but suddenly everything's upside down. Yes, Hal wants me to tell you the report came from Walter, with some circumstantial story you won't be able to check in less than a couple of days. But I've been refusing to do it that way. Either I'll tell the truth or tell you to go to hell."

"Tell the truth, Candida, it's simpler."

She shook her head shortly. "Simple is the one thing it's not. I'm honestly not trying to be clever. I don't trust you, and I'm not asking you to trust me. You can keep your eagle eye on me and see that I don't make any phone calls behind your back." She put a hand on his bare arm. "I'm in earnest. Let's sit down and do a little civilized drinking and talk about something altogether different."

Shayne was still grinning. "I knew you'd do it with a twist. And after a few civilized drinks, you wouldn't holler for help if I started unbuttoning your sweater. Isn't that part of the idea?"

"Would that be so horrible?"

"What's Begley going to be doing in the meantime?"

She ran her cool hand up his shoulder. "Conspiring, probably. Does it matter? I truly don't know what Hal has in mind. You're giving me too much credit. I merely happen to think we both need a brief intermission."

Their bodies weren't quite touching, but a steady arc of static electricity jumped the gap. Her lifted breast on the other side of the thin evening sweater touched his chest. She moved again, setting up a tiny friction and increasing the charge he was getting.

"You don't want to drink," she said. "You have only one hand. You may need it."

She took the glass and put it on the headboard. She came twisting back and drifted in against him.

"Mike," she whispered, her hand sliding around his waist. "God, I like people who—"

Shayne was thinking that there was actually nothing Begley or anyone could do during the next half hour that would make much difference. When her mouth came up, he had every intention of kissing her. At the same time, he wasn't taken by surprise when the bare arm which she was raising to slip around his neck jerked in at him suddenly, and the hand proved to have a bookend in it.

He fell away from the swing, and the bookend grazed his head. He pulled her to the floor after him. The bookend, a bronze bust of Beethoven, bounced on the carpet beside him.

He was laughing. "If you don't stop trying so hard, you'll end up with circles under your eyes."

He pulled her in against him, his hand on her bare neck, and kissed her hard. She struggled for only a moment, then gave herself to the kiss. He felt some of the tension leave her. Rotating, she slipped the rest of the way to the floor, taking him with her.

A moment passed before he raised his head. "Now maybe we understand each other. It begins to dawn on me that you aren't worried about those pictures of Despard and the girl. That's not why you tried to knock me out. What you don't want me to study is the time sheet."

She shifted, pinioned to the floor by the heavy sling. "Who told you about it? Jake? Jake, of course. I shouldn't have kept it this long. I thought we might need it for authentication."

"Doesn't United States Chemical trust you?"

"Why should they?"

"Who sold you the report? Young Hallam?"

"Mike, that cast weighs a ton. It's crushing me. Before I say yes or no, will you please think about the implications?"

"I've already thought about them."

"Then can't you see why—"

The phone rang.

CHAPTER 13

She looked up at Shayne for a moment. When the phone rang again, she replied with a low-voiced obscenity, a curt

Anglo-Saxon expletive that is not usually part of the vocabulary of nicely reared girls.

"Just when we were getting somewhere."

"Don't answer it."

"It's probably Hal. If I don't answer, he'll be back to see what's going on."

He moved the cast and let her up. She kissed the corner of his mouth lightly.

"If you can't remember where we were, I'll remind you."

"Why don't you quit him, Candida?"

"What a silly question. Tomorrow morning I become a partner and start drawing half the profits. That's pretty good for a small-town girl."

The phone had kept on ringing. She picked it up but finished what she was saying to Shayne, her hand over the mouthpiece. "And I don't need to be told what will happen if this collapses. He'll pretend he doesn't know me. That's why I hope to keep it from collapsing."

She said hello. Shayne heard the unmistakable voice of a professional operator.

"Michael Shayne?" Candida said, her eyebrows rising. "Right here."

She handed Shayne the phone. After the operator checked his identity, a man's voice said, "Hallam. I've been trying to locate you. Jose gave me this number."

"I'd better call you back," Shayne said. "Things have been happening."

"So I understand. Yes, I'd appreciate a call. I'm at the Mayflower. Let me tell you why I'm calling first, and if you have any questions, you can ask them when you get back to me. I want you to suspend operations."

Shayne said in a flat voice, "Are you sure that's what you want, Mr. Hallam?"

"Of course I'm sure!" Hallam was clearly not used to being asked this question. "I've just conferred with the lawyer who's representing us with the Patent Office, and the consensus is that we stand to lose more by legal action than we could possibly hope to gain."

"I thought there was more to it than that."

"You're quite right," his client said coldly. "Taking everything into account, balancing pros and cons, we've decided to cut our losses. Your fee, of course, will be paid in full."

"You mean provided I lay off?"

There was a moment's cautious silence. "I don't know that I care for your tone, Shayne. I brought you in at a handsome retainer to perform certain services. These services are no longer required."

Shayne held out his empty glass to Candida. "Get me another drink, baby. This is going to take a little time."

She shook her head. "I wouldn't want to miss anything. What's he doing, firing you?"

"Trying to," Shayne said. "I'm sometimes a hard man to fire."

He hadn't covered the mouthpiece. Hallam's voice put in, "I assume you intended me to hear that. Are you talking to Miss Morse? The girl who gave the orders to have you beaten up last night, if my information is correct."

"Well, she's a damned good-looking girl," Shayne said, grinning.

She acknowledged the compliment with a movement of the cigarette she had just lighted.

"Good-looking or not," Hallam snapped, "I don't consider it wise to discuss this in the hearing of a paid agent of United States Chemical. Call me back from another phone."

"I will later. I don't want to break this off. It's picking up momentum."

"And it's obvious that you've been drinking. Very well, I'll put it as simply as possible, to make sure you understand me. I'm resigning as your client. Conceivably there may be a change in management after the next board meeting. This decision may be reversed, but until then you are no longer in our employ. Do I make myself clear?"

"Clear enough," Shayne said noncommittally. "When are you coming back?"

"Tomorrow. There's nothing more I can do here. But I'd like a more definite statement of your intentions, Shayne.

You have eight thousand dollars coming, I believe. Do we mail you the check or not?"

Shayne let him wait a minute.

"Better not," he said softly and broke the connection.

"What was that all about?"Candida asked.

"You know as much about it as I do. Let's take a look at that time sheet."

"No, wait. I'm trying to think if it makes any difference to me that you no longer have a client."

"That's no problem. I can always find another. I'm thinking of what's his name?—Perkins, of United States Chemical."

She was frowning at him when the phone rang again. He offered it to her but she shook her head.

"It's probably for you."

Shayne picked it up and said hello. Jose Despard's voice answered.

"Your line's been busy. Does that mean the old man reached you?"

"Yeah, a minute ago. How did you talk him into calling me off?"

"What's that?" Despard said warily.

"He cancelled my retainer. That's his privilege. It doesn't mean I automatically drop dead."

Despard gave a low whistle. "Well, well. It wasn't my idea. Now I'm trying to figure out where this leaves me."

"You're right where you were," Shayne assured him, "except that I now have the negatives of those shots they took of you and Deedee."

Shayne heard him swallow. "How much will you take for them?"

"They're not for sale. I'm not in that business. What did you call him about, something involving his son?"

"Now how did you know that? Well, it's narrowing down. You told me to sit down and think. I went to a bar—I can't think at home. On my second brandy I remembered something about Forbes. He has certain beatnik proclivities, I don't know if you know that. Dubious connections with civil-rights pickets and the like. There's a girl. Needless to say, there's always a girl. I don't know her name, but I've dredged up something I'd completely forgotten about, that he needed money to pay for an abortion."

"Last April?" Shayne said quickly.

"No, earlier. Around the turn of the year. He took me to lunch and asked me for a loan of eight hundred dollars. The girl wanted it done in Puerto Rico. I thought eight hundred was a bit much. I sympathized, I always feel sympathetic toward a fellow sinner, but to come up with eight hundred in a hurry I'd have to sell some bonds. To put it mildly, Mrs. Despard wouldn't O.K. going into capital for an illegal operation for somebody no one in the family has ever met."

"So you didn't give him the money?"

"No. And there was another consideration. He's an only child. That has a lot to do with the scrapes he got into while he was growing up."

"What kind of scrapes?"

"Cars, girls, nothing too serious. His mother always took care of it, his father after she became sick. We finally decided he had to start toeing the line. I say 'we' because it was a family decision. My brother-in-law asked us to cooperate, and we agreed. From that point on, Forbes had to take responsibility for the things he did." A note of embarrassment entered his voice. "I know you're probably thinking I'm no person to talk, but I take my duties as a parent seriously. I have three fine kids. Getting good marks in school."

"Did his father pay for the abortion?" Shayne said impatiently.

"I called him tonight to find out. He said no. But he may not want to admit it. There's a pattern—he's constantly telling the boy he'll stake him this one last time, and then never again. I don't suppose any of this means anything? It was just an idea. I mean, if she hit him for eight hundred in December, maybe it was only the beginning."

While Despard talked, Shayne watched Candida repair her eye makeup at the mirror. She put down the little tools and picked up her lipstick.

"Where are you, Despard?" Shayne said. "I think we've got hold of something, finally."

Despard gave him the name of the bar and agreed to wait.

"One more question," Shayne said. "How long had you known Walter Langhorne?"

"All my life. My sisters were closer to him than I was, but we did the same things—picnics, dances. Now don't double back on me, Shayne. Stick to Forbes. Walter Langhorne didn't sell that report."

"We'll talk about it," Shayne said wearily.

Candida looked across at him as he hung up. "You're still working?"

"Yeah," he said thoughtfully, rubbing his jaw.

"The Mike Shayne I've always heard about," she said, "doesn't make a move without being paid in advance."

"I expect to be paid."

She threw her lipstick in her bag. "I hate to think how close I came to telling you every last thing you wanted to know. I was so mixed up I felt like three different people. The truth is, we perform a valuable function. Big corporations like Despard have a huge and unfair advantage, with their great wealth, their control of the market. We've managed to help a few obscure companies to survive, Hal and I— I don't think that's necessarily so wicked. Well, I've changed my mind five times in five minutes, but this is definite. You and I are on opposite teams, and let's keep it that way."

"The sex wasn't my idea."

"Oh, I'm terrible. Seducing a man with only one arm to fight me off. I'll iron your shirt."

She went into the bathroom and came back with his damp shirt. She unfolded an ironing board. She added in a low voice without looking at him, "Not that I didn't think it was going very nicely."

Shayne laughed openly. "The hell you did. You were thinking of too many other things at the same time. Where will you be if anything comes up?"

"Right here. I have to wait for a call from Hal. What

could come up? Your terms are unconditional surrender, and I've decided to take my chances."

She worked on the shirt for only a moment. "For some reason you make me nervous, Mike. It'll have to dry on you."

She tossed it to him. When she saw how hard it was to put on, she came to help him, which brought her back within the radius of his good arm. As soon as the shirt was on and the sling adjusted she stepped back quickly.

"You have an appointment. Please. Go. If you stay another thirty seconds, I'll change my mind again. That would be ridiculous, wouldn't it?"

CHAPTER 14

Shayne had made it clear that he was going somewhere else. Candida had made it equally clear that she was staying home.

Shayne moved his Buick to a less conspicuous parking lot on the other side of Alhambra Circle, one reserved for University of Miami faculty. From here he had an unobstructed view of the exit from Candida's little court, and he could leave quickly in either direction.

He killed his headlights.

A moment or so later a black Ford with a buggy-whip aerial cruised past. It looked to Shayne like a City of Miami police car. The driver was peering into parked cars. As he passed under a streetlight Shayne recognized him. It was Vince Camilli, the vice cop who had raided Deedee's apartment.

Camilli's head had swiveled toward Shayne's Buick. His brake lights flared. Shayne thought fast. He was carrying only one thing that would make trouble for him with a vice cop—the blackmail negatives, showing Deedee and Jose Despard at four stages in the presumed rape. The one Shayne had looked at had been relatively innocuous, but the others were undoubtedly worse.

Camilli left the Ford double-parked with its headlights on full. Shayne whipped the envelope containing the negatives out of his pocket and tried to slip it under the floor covering. But he had to crouch low to reach the edge of the rubber pad with his right hand, and Camilli saw him straighten.

Shayne flicked on the switch of a battery-powered tape recorder under the front seat as the other approached. Camilli, chewing gum, his thumbs hooked in his belt, was moving at the easy saunter used by cops when they believe they are about to make a high-prestige arrest and their quarry has little chance to get away from them.

"Mike Shayne again," he said lazily. "You get around, for a man with a bad arm. What are you doing on University property, may I ask?"

"You can ask," Shayne said evenly. "What are you doing in Coral Gables? You're out of your jurisdiction here."

"Let's not worry about that. Ever since I saw you tonight, I've been thinking about some of those uncalled-for remarks of yours about frame-ups. Somebody's a hooker, or a flagrant fag. Everybody knows it. They're guilty as hell, and we can't bring them in unless we catch them in the act. Well?" He jerked the door open. "What did you just stick under the front seat?"

"Where's your partner?"

"He was in the john," Camilli said. "When the call came in and I heard Mike Shayne was involved, I didn't wait. I moved."

He had a long three-cell flashlight in one hand. Shayne shifted his feet, untying the knot of the sling with a quick pull. As Camilli leaned forward, his jowls were on a direct line with the hidden knuckles. Shayne suppressed an impulse to jerk his elbow outward. Camilli was a cop, after all. A good way to get in trouble in any town, including this one, was to slug cops.

As Camilli's right hand entered the beam of light, Shayne

saw that he was holding his thumb folded under against the palm. Without further thought, Shayne broke the scalpel loose from the plaster and lifted the cast over Camilli's hulking shoulders. He dug the hook in the back of his jacket and yanked him forward, at the same time bringing the bright razor-sharp edge of the scalpel up toward his throat.

Camilli made a choking sound. He tried to pull back, but the hook held him.

"Open your hand," Shayne ordered.

Camilli merely gurgled. Shayne repeated the command and nicked off a small slice of his chin with a pass of the scalpel. The cop's eyes protruded dangerously. Slowly he turned his hand over. A brown, amateurish-looking cigarette slid to the floor beneath the steering column.

Shayne clucked. "I see you were going to pull me in for possession. You get into habits and they're hard to break. Where did the call come from, Camilli?"

Camilli's voice was thin and high. "You won't use that shiv. You're too smart. I'm a police officer!"

"I keep reminding myself," Shayne said. "I'll ask you again, and I'm still asking you nicely. Where did the call come from?"

Blood dripped from Camilli's chin. He tried to swallow, but nothing went down.

"Washington," he whispered, his eyes on the bright blade.

"Washington," Shayne repeated without expression. "I'm glad you decided to tell me. They're new seat covers. I wouldn't like to get blood all over them. Go on."

"Mike, for God's sake, do you know what you're doing? You can't control your arm. One touch with that thing—"

Shayne's hand with the scalpel was rock-steady an inch in front of his chin.

"Said his name was Hallam," Camilli gasped. "He fired you, you were trying to extort money from him. Please. Will you please, Mike? That wasn't enough to hold you on. The reefer was only a gag! He said if you were out of the way for twenty-four hours, he'd give me a check for my favorite charity."

"Which one is that," Shayne inquired, "the Society for the Advancement of Vince Camilli? Straighten up slowly and turn around."

He relaxed the pull of the hook and Camilli straightened. The scalpel followed him up and out of the car. Shayne freed the hook. Then, dropping the scalpel into his pocket, he slid his hand under Camilli's arm and got his gun. He scaled it across the lot beneath the next line of parked cars. Using the blunt end of the hook, he walked him across the street to his Ford.

There Shayne reached in and sliced the main battery cable. He allowed Camilli to turn to face him, and cut his belt with a quick upward stroke of the scalpel. Camilli grabbed at his pants as they fell.

"Get in," Shayne said. "The thing for you to do now is get your retirement papers in before tomorrow morning. If you move fast, I may not mention that stick of marijuana to anybody. I want you out of Miami inside a week."

"Mike, I've got roots here—I own a house—"

"Sell it," Shayne said. "Shaking down whores is one thing. This is something else. I've got that conversation on tape. All I need to do is make a couple of calls."

He motioned with the scalpel and Camilli fell into the front seat. Shayne turned his back on him and returned to the Buick without looking around.

An instant after the door of the Buick slammed, a red Volkswagen scurried out of Candida's court and turned north on Alhambra Circle.

Shayne wasted a second or two getting underway. The Volkswagen was already blinking for a right at Blue Road. There was no doubt in his mind that she must be going north. That was where the action was tonight. He continued across, turning into Bird Road at the end of the next long block. Here he gunned his powerful motor, crossed Granada Boulevard on the tail end of a green light, and hit seventy-five by the time he braked for Route One.

The red Volkswagen came into sight. As it went through the intersection, Shayne had a glimpse of Candida. She was driving intently, her hands high on the wheel.

From there it was easy. She crossed to Miami Beach

on the Venetian Causeway. Shayne was the second car behind as she stopped to pay the toll. After passing Municipal Park on the Beach, she turned onto Collins, the street of the great hotels.

If she was about to turn, she would be watching her mirror, and Shayne dropped back. His timing was bad. Caught by a red light, he picked up the phone.

When the operator came on, he told her to hold. Ahead, the Volkswagen swung into the long curving approach to the St. Albans. Still immobilized by the light, Shayne gave the operator the St. Albans number. A moment later he was asking for the security man, Harry Hurlbut.

"Hurlbut," a voice said.

"Mike Shayne, in a hurry. I know you like to be in on things. I have a strong feeling something's about to happen."

Hurlbut groaned. "Why here? Why not at the Fontainebleu?"

"A girl's going to be along in a minute. Can you see the main-lobby entrance from your office?"

"Wait a minute," his friend told him. "Yeah, now I can."

"I can't follow her in. I want to know what she does—it could make a big difference. She's a blonde. Red skirt, sleeveless sweater, no hat. She's alone."

"Right," Hurlbut said alertly. "I think she just came in now. Sweater buttons in front, all the way up."

The light changed. Shayne wedged the phone between his shoulder and jaw. After crossing the intersection, he turned into the approach to the St. Albans.

"She's using a house phone," Hurlbut said. "I'll get the board."

He clicked off. Shayne fitted the Buick into an opening at the curb. In a moment Hurlbut was back.

"She's calling twelve-sixteen. They're still ringing. Still ringing. Wait a minute, I'll check the register."

After another brief pause Hurlbut said, "I thought that was the room. Ruth Di Palma. Mike, you'll have to tell me more about this before I go any farther."

"You know the girl?"

"I know her."

"How about a Forbes Hallam, Jr., do you know him?"

"I don't think so. Is he a guest here?"

"No. Still no answer?"

He waited. Hurlbut reported: "No answer. She hung up. There's no back to that sweater! Jesus, that's a really gorgeous number. She's getting a magazine at the stand. Sitting down. I enjoy having girls like that in my lobby. They add to the decor. Go on."

"There's not a hell of a lot more I can tell you," Shayne said. "Hallam tried to raise some money about a year ago so his girl could get an abortion. I don't know her name but the indications are that it's this Di Palma girl. I need to find out if he got up the money, and where it came from. I also may be totally wrong about the whole thing."

"That doesn't happen too often, Mike. The thing is, this girl is damn nice. By that I mean *damn* nice. I've had a couple of dates with her myself. Anything I tell you about her, you'll get the wrong idea. We make her a rate because she knows everybody in town. Her friends tend to be good swimmers and divers with a year-round tan and it helps the pool. You know the tourist-hotel business. By the time people can afford our rates, they're fat and bald. That doesn't mean they want to spend their vacation in a hotel where everybody else is fat and bald, especially in bathing suits. Do you want to see her?"

"It would help."

"I think I can find her for you. She's at what they call a 'soul session.' You know? The papers are spreading the idea it's a new kind of orgy, but it's just a bunch of people with problems, and who doesn't have problems nowadays? Ruthie wanted to know if they could have it here. I said why not, but the brass vetoed it—by the end of a long weekend everybody's looking pretty grubby. I suggested the Stanwick, the new motel in Surfside. If you want to hold on, I can check. They'll be breaking about now."

Shayne told him to go ahead. He listened to a dead phone for several minutes. Then Hurlbut was back.

"Yeah—the Stanwick. Room twenty-four. You'll recognize her. She's got a great build. A short haircut—pretty near white."

"Thanks, Harry. Keep an eye on the blonde for me."

"A pleasure, especially from the rear. The thing about these backless fashions—you can't help wondering what they've got on in front."

Shayne hung up and went around the semicircle back to Collins.

CHAPTER 15

The Stanwick Motel had been in place for a season and a half, and it was looking a little seedy. One letter was gone from its neon sign. Its four floors were arranged around three sides of a lighted swimming pool. The pool was closed for the night.

Shayne found room 24 without trouble. It was one of a suite of three connecting rooms, and all the rooms along that gallery were dark. Apparently the organizers of the weekend had been talked into renting the entire section to avoid disturbing the other guests.

Shayne opened the door and walked in. His arrival went unnoticed by the six or seven people in the room. On one bed, a man with a magnificent head of white hair was weeping silently. A man and a girl, on opposite sides of a TV set, stared at each other as though they had never seen anything so strange and fascinating. The man was talking in a low monotone which gave an effect of extreme excitement.

Shayne stepped over the outstretched legs of a middle-aged Negro woman, several hours past the point of complete exhaustion, and continued into the next room. A young girl was studying her reflection in a mirror. Her lips moved silently; she was probably telling herself some home truths. In the third room, several people, including the girl Shayne had come to see, were attending closely to a discussion between two men and a much older woman. Shayne tuned in briefly. The older woman, it seemed, was being accused of playing a role in some kind of psychological game involving herself and the two men, but she was refusing to acknowledge that any such game existed or that she was a part of it. Probably, Shayne thought, if he had been present all Saturday and Sunday he would have understood why the exhausted audience was following the exchange with such interest.

He had spotted Ruth Di Palma the minute he came in. She was lying on her stomach on one of the beds, her chin on a doubled pillow, her eyes jumping from one speaker to the next. Her sun-whitened hair was very close-cropped. Her tan was excellent. She was wearing tight slacks, a shapeless sweatshirt, no makeup.

Shayne ripped the flyleaf from a Gideon Bible, scribbled "Can I talk to you?" on it, and slipped it inside the leather folder containing his detective's license. He touched the girl on the shoulder with it.

The surface of her eyes as she looked up at him was opaque with fatigue. She took in his sling, then she looked again at his face. There could have been either hostility or indifference in her eyes.

After reading the note and glancing at the license, she commented with a slight upward movement of an eyebrow and rolled off the bed. She was barefooted, and not tall. She seemed to be smoldering quietly, and it was probably this quality, Shayne thought, that had impressed Hurlbut, a hard man to impress.

Shayne opened the door. They went out to the gallery without passing through the other two rooms.

"What time is it?" she asked.

Shayne told her and she said, "It's about time we knock off." She stifled a dry yawn. "I'm tired, and at the same time I'm not. Pills and coffee, coffee and pills. And I think that's a different kind of oxygen we've been breathing in there."

"Half cigarette smoke," he said.

She put both hands on the gallery rail and breathed in deeply. Her face had a strained look, a look Shayne associated with the amphetamines, or stay-awake pills.

"Your Georgia weekend didn't work out?"

"It was over before it started," Shayne told her. "Long ago now."

"That was my prediction. You don't get results from one of these things by pushing. If it comes, it comes."

"You know what we were trying to find out?"

"Forbes hasn't been talking about much else."

Shayne offered her a cigarette. She shook her head. He lit one himself and said, "People are trying to convince me he's been peddling his company's secrets. What do you think?"

"I try not to think about dull subjects." She drew another deep breath, so deep it seemed to make her dizzy. "Or do you want me to act surprised?"

"I thought you might react one way or another."

She turned toward him, apparently looking at him for the first time with a flicker of interest. "Whether Company A or Company B brings out a new paint first means very little to me."

"Does it make any difference to you whether or not Forbes is a thief?"

"That's a fine distinction I can't get excited about. I understand why it interests you—it's your business."

"He could go to jail."

"Don't be silly. He's the heir apparent. They wouldn't let it get that far. They'd simply act hurt and drop him from the payroll. And if you really want my opinion, which I sort of doubt, that's the best thing that could happen to Forbes."

"So he could spend his time writing?"

"So he could spend his time getting something to write about."

Shayne was trying to decide how much of this was real, and how much the result of the sleepless weekend. For an instant she seemed to be touched by an ordinary human worry.

"I doubt if he did it," she said abruptly. "I think that foolish job means more to him than he pretends—it's a flaw in his character. He denies it, but he plays by different rules between Monday and Friday."

"Can you tell me anything about his finances?"

"What do you want to know? He's trying to live on his salary, and he's suffering. You'd be astonished to hear how little they pay him. It's the barest minimum. Under our Friday-to-Monday rules, he's not supposed to think about money every minute. I'm afraid I'm giving him premature ulcers."

"Did you ask him for money last December or January for a trip to Puerto Rico?"

She gave a low, warm laugh. "Who told you about that? His father?"

"His uncle."

"Well, Mr. Shayne, I'll admit I asked him. But don't let it blow up out of proportion. I didn't know him well then. I asked him to pay for an abortion I didn't actually need. I was broke and I wanted to go to Puerto Rico. I didn't know he was getting starvation wages."

Shayne flicked cigarette ash over the railing. "Did you go to Puerto Rico in the end?"

"Of course."

"Does Forbes know you were faking about the abortion?"

"I told him later. He didn't like it, which is what I mean. He cares about that kind of thing."

She stretched all over, like a cat. She had a cat's sleekness and indifference, and she was equally finely muscled. "He's coming to pick me up. Does he know you're hot on the trail?"

Shayne suddenly felt a surge of anger. Taking her by the shoulder, he pulled her around roughly and made her look at him. "Don't you realize he's in trouble?"

"But it's not the kind of trouble I care about, you see. I don't love Forbes. I've been careful not to, and sometimes it took a certain force of character, because he has possibilities. But I'm not going to wade up to my neck in glop, just to fit in with somebody else's ideas."

"What the hell are you talking about?"

"If you really want to know," she said quietly, "I like your hand on my shoulder. It's started the machinery. The one thing I don't like about the men I know is that not many of them are men. If you want to rent a room for us here—it's Sunday night, I'm sure there are vacancies—fine. I think we'd enjoy ourselves. But if Forbes found out about it, he'd be morose for days. He's a permanent type. I'm not. I could copy a paint formula and hawk it from door to door, because what earthly difference would it make? Forbes couldn't."

Shayne gave an unwilling laugh and let her go. "You've convinced me. That's what you wanted to do, wasn't it?"

She took his face in both hands and kissed him on the mouth. "Think what you like. But I'm willing to go to that room if you want to, for as long as you want to stay."

He looked into her eyes. "I know your name and your St. Albans room number. Right now I'm working."

She nodded gravely, and after a moment she went back into the room.

CHAPTER 16

Shayne was waiting in his Buick, on his third cigarette, when Forbes Hallam, Jr., zoomed into the parking lot in his low-slung black Jaguar.

The door didn't entirely latch as he got out. He took the outer steps two at a time and disappeared. A few minutes later Ruth came back with him. She was still barefoot, carrying a pair of sandals by their straps. She leaned her head against his shoulder as they came down the stairs. There was a long, deep kiss in the Jaguar before they got underway.

Shayne followed them south to Miami Beach.

He had checked the St. Albans twice by phone. The security man told him Candida Morse was still waiting. Shayne wanted to be present at this meeting, and as soon as Forbes committed the Jaguar to the St. Albans approach, he swung his Buick into the unmarked drive leading to the ramp to the service entrance. He leaped out at the unloading platform and entered the hotel through the kitchens.

He was in the ornate lobby before Forbes and the girl came in the main entrance.

Candida, he saw, was sitting near the archway into the Blue Bar, idly turning the pages of a magazine. He moved closer. From a vantage point behind a huge bronze statue of a mother and child, he saw an unmistakable sharpening of her attention as she noticed the other two. She slowly turned a page. They passed with no sign of recognition.

Ruth had put on her sandals. Her face was still bare of makeup. Even in the baggy sweatshirt she was the most exciting girl within Shayne's range of vision, with the possible exception of Candida, who had the advantage of taking a sensible interest in money. Ruth and Forbes were holding hands. Again, as they waited for an elevator, her head dropped against his shoulder. He smiled down at her and said something that made her laugh.

As soon as an elevator took them out of sight, Candida put her magazine aside and checked her appearance in a pocket mirror. She did something minor to her hair. She looked at her watch. After a moment she uncrossed her elegant legs and stood up. She looked at the titles in a paperback rack, studied the schedule of the day's events in the hotel, and forced herself to smoke a cigarette all the way through before going to the house phones. She checked her watch again and waited another moment. After giving them five minutes together, she finally picked up the phone.

Shayne was frowning. Harry Hurlbut, a tough, pockmarked ex-middleweight, was standing in the door of his office across the lobby. Candida put the phone down and entered an empty elevator.

As soon as the door closed on her, Shayne crossed to Hurlbut's office.

"God knows what's going on, Harry," he said, puzzled. "I thought I had things figured out, but apparently not."

"Keep trying, Mike," Hurlbut said in his gravelly voice. "Whatever it is, let's control it."

"We've had a certain amount of violence, and I've been expecting some more. There's a hell of a lot of money in the game. But tonight everybody's being very well behaved."

"Please God they stay that way," Hurlbut said. "Would it help if I tell Ruthie we need her room?"

Shayne rubbed his jaw. "Harry, I just don't know. This thing has more twists than a corkscrew. I think I have to go up and throw a little weight around."

"Do it gently, will you, Mike? If you have to splash anybody off the walls, take them outside."

Shayne returned to the elevators and waited. An elevator arrived. Forbes was in it.

He looked at Shayne blankly. Shayne put his arm into the electronic field to keep the door from closing.

"It's no coincidence, Forbes. I followed you here from the Stanwick. I need to talk to you. Let's go in the bar and have a drink. After that I may have some questions to ask Miss Di Palma."

Forbes finally pushed off from the back wall. "She's been on benzedrine all weekend and she took a couple of pills to knock herself out. I'm the one you want to talk to. I've been wondering how long it would take you to get around to me."

"Yeah, I've been getting pushes in your direction," Shayne said.

At the entrance to the Blue Bar he called Hurlbut over and introduced the two men.

"When the blonde comes down, tell her I want to see her in the bar," Shayne said. "Maybe we can settle everything peaceably."

"Knock on wood."

Shayne took Forbes into the bar, found a large enough opening on a banquette and ordered drinks.

"I'm sorry about the arm, Mike," Forbes said in a low

voice. "I know it's part of your profession, but I'm sorry just the same."

"I'll sue somebody," Shayne said. "Did you know your father fired me?"

Forbes swung around in surprise. "What did he do that for? Did you insult him or something? We've only got one more day."

"He's writing it off," Shayne told him. "He says he'd rather take a small money loss than look dumb in public. I think he's really afraid I'm onto something that will lead to a family scandal or endanger his control of the company. He put a cop on me to make sure I was paying attention."

"I thought he was in Washington."

"They have phones in Washington. He happened to be talking to a cop who could take a hint."

The drinks arrived. Shayne raised his. Forbes was thinking about something else. When he saw that Shayne was waiting, he started and picked up his drink.

"Cheers," he said gloomily. "He's trying to cover up for me, I guess. Who told him?"

"Your Uncle Jose. He wanted to know if your father ended up paying for Ruth's abortion."

"Oh, that," Forbes said, his face clearing. "That turned out to be nothing. She made a mistake."

"How much money was involved? I was told eight hundred."

"That's right. Dad loaned me some money the year before to cover a payment I had to make because of an accident. A hit-and-run thing, except I didn't know I hit anybody. I didn't have eight hundred. I'd only been going with Ruth a few months. She thought, on the basis of the Jaguar, the job, my rich family, she thought all I had to do was reach for the money clip and peel off hundred-dollar bills until she told me to stop. She knows better now. It turned out nobody considered me much of a credit risk. I was beginning to think I'd have to ask for offers on the Jag. I wanted to leave Dad out of this one if possible. Jose told him. Dad yelled a bit, but finally he said he'd take care of it. Then Ruthie came up with the good news—false alarm."

Shayne drank some cognac and followed it with a sip of ice water. "That was the winter crisis. Now how about the spring one?"

Forbes sighed. "I knew you'd pick it up. That was worse. That was so bad it still gives me the shivers. This time it was ten thousand."

"For another abortion?"

"Mike, you have the wrong idea about Ruthie. I'm not sore, just explaining. She had a letter from dumb me taking full credit for the baby. She could have made me marry her or come through with a big settlement. Mother was sick at the time, and there was a family theory that the news would be bad for her. Good God, I *want* to marry Ruthie. She's the one who won't marry me. No, this ten-thousand deal was something else, an old bane of mine. Stud poker."

Shayne's manner was offhand, but his grip on the cognac glass tightened. "That's a lot of dough to drop in a poker game."

"I'm aware of the fact," Forbes said sadly. "It went on all night and all the next day. Talk about soul sessions. At one point I was fourteen thousand ahead."

"Who was the big winner?"

"A fellow from New York, Lou Johnson. There's something I want to explain, Mike. Someday I'd like to do a novel about these people, these friends of Ruthie's. It's material nobody else has used. They're"—he made a rippling gesture with one hand—"I don't know, floaters. They go where the wind takes them. They're talented enough to do anything they want to, except that they don't want to do anything. I really think I can catch the style. I admit I was drunk when I lost that money. But once I got involved in that high-stake poker game, I wanted to go all the way—for the book, you see? And of course, Mother was in the back of my mind all the time. If I dropped a few thousand, I knew she'd make it good, she always had. Well, she died a week later."

He closed his eyes. "I'm posing again. I don't suppose I'll ever write that book."

"Send me a copy if you do," Shayne said dryly. "What business is Lou Johnson in?"

"Oh, he has something to do with raising money for the theater. He's affable enough, and at the same time he's a little scarey, somehow."

"There wouldn't be any point in losing to him otherwise," Shayne observed.

"You may be right. I wish I didn't have to be such a fool."

"If your mother had lived, would she have covered you to the extent of ten grand?"

"No. They would have settled for less. They agreed to come down fifty percent as it was."

"Who agreed?"

"Johnson sent two friends to see me. One of them held me while the other hit me. Then they switched. I don't stand pain well. I faced that fact about myself long ago. They told me they'd be back a week later for the five thousand."

"Who did you ask for it?"

"Walter first. I knew he had it. I wanted to give him a lien on my share of Mother's estate. He turned me down. I'm sure it was Dad's doing. Then Dad turned me down, in no uncertain terms. I invented a reason to go out to the Coast. I stayed away a few weeks. I'd probably still be out there, but I found out that Johnson had been arrested in New York on some kind of narcotics charge. I decided to come back and I'm glad I did. Those two characters never came near me again."

Shayne saw Candida hestitating in the doorway. He signaled to her. She stood irresolutely for another moment, then made up her mind and came over.

"I was under the impression we said goodnight a couple of hours ago, Mike."

"I waited around to see if you really stayed home," he said. "You know Forbes Hallam."

"No, I don't," she said evenly. "Candida Morse. How do you do?"

Forbes had risen. "The Hal Begley Miss Morse? I don't know what I expected. Something different."

Shayne waved to a waiter. "She tells me she's in it for the excitement, not the money. What are you drinking, Candida?"

"Nothing, thank you. I shouldn't even have come in here, but curiosity got the better of me. I suppose you're talking about our one big subject."

"What else?"

They sat down. Shayne ordered a new round of drinks.

"Forbes has been telling me how he was maneuvered into needing five thousand bucks in a hurry last April. We're moving on to the next question. Who did the maneuvering?"

Candida looked at him levelly, then turned to the waiter. "I think I'll have a Scotch and soda."

Forbes protested, "Nobody planned it, Mike. I get in my own jams, from sheer natural stupidity."

"Not this time," Shayne said. "You were playing against a stacked deck. The timing was too good. Candida, do you know a New York gambler named Lou Johnson?"

"I don't know any New York gamblers."

"How early in the year did you get the United States contract?"

She felt for cigarettes, considering her answer while she took one out and Shayne lighted it for her.

"I don't want to make your job any easier, Mike. Maybe you can provoke me into saying something, but I hope to be able to keep my mouth shut."

"My guess would be early or mid-March," Shayne said. "After you listened to my end of that Washington call from Forbes's father, why did you head straight for the St. Albans and wait an hour or so for Ruth to show up? I think you probably wanted to give her money to get out of town."

Forbes exclaimed, "Miss Morse, you and Ruthie know each other?"

Candida gathered her loose belongings and stuffed them in her bag. "This was a mistake, I see. I won't wait for the Scotch. Goodnight, all."

"No, stick around," Shayne advised her. "There's even a

faint chance that you're being taken here—a very faint chance. When did your mother die, Forbes?"

"April second."

"The poker game was a week earlier. Candida was already sounding out Walter Langhorne on the subject of changing jobs. A blackmail operation was underway against Jose Despard. Which of these three gambits actually produced the T-239 folder I still don't know. When did the two collectors come to see you, Forbes? I'd say about the twentieth. Suddenly, on April twenty-third, you no longer needed five G's. You can't really think anything as elaborate as this would be called off just because one of the principals was picked up in New York on another matter. There had to be a payoff. It doesn't make sense otherwise."

Forbes nodded slowly. "I think I know what happened, Mike. I've tried not to think about it. I think my father quietly bought up those IOU's. After that abortion thing, he made one of his announcements. From that moment on, I had to get out of trouble on my own two feet. But he knew what would happen if I didn't pay that five thousand. I was in for a really bad beating, and something like that can easily get out of hand. He wanted to make me realize that life isn't easy. He didn't want me killed."

The waiter brought their drinks and Shayne asked for a phone.

"You don't want to comment on this yet, Candida?"

She drank without replying.

When the phone was plugged in, he dialed the long-distance combination and asked for Washington information.

Forbes sat forward. "Dad won't like being asked about it, I can tell you that."

"That's too bad."

He asked the operator for the number of the Hotel Mayflower and started his new drink while he waited. A moment or two later Hallam's father was on the line.

"Shayne!" he exclaimed when he was told who was calling.

"Camilli decided not to arrest me," Shayne said. "He's

putting in for retirement instead. Something's come up that has to do with your son, Mr. Hallam."

"Don't tell me about it!" Hallam snapped. "You no longer have any legal right to ask members of my family or executives of my company any questions whatever on any subject."

"That's pretty sweeping," Shayne said mildly. "Forbes is right here. Do you want to talk to him?"

"Put him on."

Forbes took the phone, holding it as though it might go off in his hands. "Dad, do you remember those stupid IOU's I was worrying about last spring? We want to find out if you—"

His father interrupted. The harsh rasp in his voice carried to Shayne without forming any recognizable words.

"But Dad," Forbes said, "if you did buy them that would—"

His father broke in again, giving him no chance to say anything more. The electronic rasp continued for some time, concluding with an audible click. Forbes looked at the phone, puzzled.

"He said not to talk to you. He's flying back. He says you're after more money."

"He offered me eight thousand to quit," Shayne said. "I don't think anybody else will top that. Now I have to ask you the yes-or-no question, Forbes. Did you sell the folder to Candida?"

"No."

But there was no conviction in his voice, as though this detail was of no interest to him. After a long swallow of whiskey, he burst out, "I don't see why I shouldn't talk to you! My God, we can't just expect you to—"

"He doesn't want you to incriminate yourself," Shayne said. "When we check on it, I think we'll find that Lou Johnson or somebody acting for Lou Johnson received the full five thousand, and if it didn't come from your father, the assumption would be that it came from you. But there's one other outside possibility—that there's a third person involved, who really stole the folder and set up the poker game so you'd take the fall if it ever got that close."

"That's nonsense."

"I think Candida would have been willing to go as high as thirty or forty thousand for that material. A five-thousand-buck payoff to Johnson would be cheap insurance."

Forbes rattled the ice in his drink. He shook his head. "Johnson was Ruthie's friend. She knew he was staying in the hotel, and it was her idea to get in the game. In fact—"

"In fact what?" Shayne said when he stopped.

"It seems to me she suggested taking off the limit, and that's when the trouble started. I'm not sure of that part, but if somebody introduced her to Johnson—hell, maybe she collected a small percentage, I've never been able to make out where her money comes from. But if somebody arranged that game to get my signature on some IOU's, she knows who it was. We can find out in the morning."

Shayne drained his glass and stood up. "We'd better ask her now. She may be many miles away in the morning."

"She's asleep."

"Maybe not. She was pretty strung out when I saw her. The sleeping pills wouldn't take hold right away. Coming, Candida?"

"Needless to say, for my own protection."

Shayne overpaid the waiter and hurried the others to the elevator. He and Harry Hurlbut exchanged a look, and the elevator door slid shut. They rode up in unfriendly silence. On the twelfth floor, Forbes led them to Ruth's room.

Shayne knocked. When there was no immediate response, he said, "Keep knocking. I'll get a key."

"I have one."

Forbes unlocked the door. "Ruthie?" he called softly. He turned to Shayne. "I told you she's asleep."

"Maybe we can wake her up."

Shayne turned on the ceiling light. This room was like

most other hotel rooms in Miami Beach—a low ceiling, walls painted light green, furniture and fixtures modern, clean-lined and anonymous. But Ruth Di Palma was an exceptionally untidy guest. Her clothes were everywhere. Slacks and sweatshirt were crumpled in the middle of the carpet. Sandals and underclothing made a trail toward the bathroom. A damp footprint had been left on the carpet by a bare foot, beside a wet bathtowel. There was a glass of water and an open bottle of pills on the bedside table, with a spilled cigarette package, a sheaf of bills and other odds and ends from Ruth's open bag.

Ruth herself was sleeping face down in the untidy bed, breathing hard. She was unclothed. Her midsection was covered by a corner of the sheet.

"We're wasting our time," Forbes said. "She never gets to sleep right away, but once she makes it—"

Shayne reached the bed in two strides. He touched the flesh at the corner of the girl's mouth. Dropping to one knee, he felt for the wrist that was dangling over the side. For a moment he couldn't find a pulse. Her breath caught and held, caught and held. He finally picked up a pulse-beat. It was faint and ragged.

He grabbed the phone, knocking her opened bag to the floor.

"Get a doctor up here in a hurry!" he said urgently when the switchboard answered.

CHAPTER 17

She died at 1:30 the next morning.

Shayne and the others were waiting in an unoccupied room across the hall. Hurlbut summoned Shayne out to the hall with a movement of his head.

"Goddamn it, Mike," Hurlbut said in a savage undertone. "Fifteen minutes earlier and they think we could have saved her. She had looks, good health, brains, friends—why do they do it?"

Shayne lit a cigarette. "You think it was suicide?"

"That's how it looks. We'll have to go to an autopsy to find out. It's either that or an accident—too much liquor and too many different pills. They had a case like it at the Sans Souci last week. I didn't think she looked too bombed when she came through the lobby."

"She's been taking bennies all weekend to stay awake."

The security man swore under his breath. "I really liked that kid, Mike."

Shayne entered the room where the girl had died. She still lay on the bed, covered by the sheet. A Mt. Sinai interne was dismantling the resuscitator. The hotel doctor, a tired-looking man Shayne didn't know, was closing his case at the bureau. Ruth's sweatshirt was still in the middle of the carpet. It had been walked on.

Shayne went over to the doctor. "My name's Michael Shayne. This girl's part of a case I'm working on. I know you can't give me a definite cause of death, but are there any indications one way or another?"

The doctor finished what he was doing. He was a young man, going bald. "You know better than that, Shayne. Wait for the autopsy."

He went into the bathroom to wash his hands. Shayne was waiting when he came out. The doctor said angrily, "Is it important?"

"Damn important."

The doctor buttoned his shirt collar and tightened the knot of his necktie. He went to the bedside, where he turned down the sheet and lifted the dead girl's left arm. Turning her wrist, he showed Shayne several spidery red lines.

"A prior attempt? Maybe. Several years ago, I'd say. I don't know the girl, never been my patient. I think it's a case of barbiturate poisoning, twenty-five grains minimum. No signs of alcohol complication. Half-empty prescription bottle, wrist scars. What does it look like to you? But I'd like it better if she'd left a note. People are so used to having pills around, they get careless."

He looked down at Ruth's face. Her expression was peaceful, not much changed from the way it had been in life.

"Not knowing what she had on her mind," the doctor said, "I have to say it's a tossup. Look at the room, the mess in that handbag. Not an orderly person, but the kind of person who would lose count and swallow too many pills accidentally?" He broke off. "The hell with it. I can't help you. Talk to the medical examiner. Now I'm going to bed."

He raised the sheet.

Shayne thanked him and stood at the bedside for a moment thinking, while the interne wheeled the resuscitator out of the room. Hurlbut came in, looked at Shayne's preoccupied face, and went out again with the doctor.

Alone with the dead girl, Shayne began to move about restlessly, trying to put together an impression of Ruth Di Palma from the scattered personal objects amid the impersonal hotel furniture. There was only one book in the room, a paperback by a Protestant clergyman, known for his advice to lonely and unhappy people who dreamed of improving their chances in life without going back to infancy to start over. The binding was badly sprung, and sections had been read more than once.

The objects on the bedside table had been returned to the girl's bag. Shayne emptied the bag again and picked over the contents. He did a careful job, trying to force each object to disclose its secrets before putting it back in the bag. Presently he was left with a curiously-designed pill container. It was flat and circular. The pills were arranged around the circumference of a movable calendar wheel, in sockets numbered from one to twenty.

After studying this for a long moment he dropped it in his pocket and went back to the hall, where Hurlbut was conferring with the doctor. When they were through, Shayne arranged for the use of the room across the hall for the remainder of the night.

He went in. Candida was smoking in one of the two

chairs, one leg over the chair arm. She looked at Shayne without expression.

"What do they think?"

Shayne poured a drink from a cognac bottle supplied earlier by Room Service. Forbes was outside on the terrace, leaning over the railing looking out at the ocean. His back was stiff.

Without raising his voice Shayne said, "Come in now, Forbes. We have things to talk about."

Forbes turned. His eyes were red and puffy.

"What things?"

"Come in and sit down."

Forbes did as he was told, moving jerkily.

"Your father's right about one thing," Shayne told him. "It's time for you to start taking a little responsibility. You don't realize it yet, but this is your worst jam to date."

"What do you mean?"

"You're feeling sorry for yourself because your girl's dead. I'm sorry too, sorry she let herself get mixed up with you people. Candida, are you going to stick to your story that you never met Forbes before tonight?"

"It's true."

"Maybe you can convince me of that, but not without doing a certain amount of talking. Here's how things stand at the moment. Ruth may have attempted suicide a few years ago. There are scars on her wrist."

"She got those in a car accident," Forbes put in.

"Forbes," Shayne said patiently, "if you have any sense at all, you won't say one more word until I'm finished. She could have been lying to explain the scars. What I'm trying to tell you is that the doctor assumes this was another suicide attempt, only this one succeeded. The autopsy will probably bear that out. But I'm ninety-nine-percent certain that when she went to sleep she expected to wake up again. Here's why I think so."

He held out the pill wheel to Candida. "Do you know what these are? They were in her purse."

She glanced at them. "Birth-control pills. Druggists don't ask to see a marriage license before they fill that prescription."

"Take a closer look."

She took the wheel and studied it. When she spoke there was an undercurrent of excitement in her voice.

"Last night's pill is gone."

"So?" Forbes demanded.

"The idea is with these things," Shayne explained, "you have to be careful not to miss a day. You build up immunity over a period—five days, I think it is, five days running. So for girls like Ruth, who might forget, they're packaged this way. You buy them by the month. When you take the first pill in a new cycle, you turn the wheel to that day's date and lock it. As you work your way through the month, you always know where you are."

"I still don't see—" Forbes said.

"Use your head, damn it!" Shayne said sharply. "Ruth's in bed. She's decided to kill herself, so she won't have to get up in the morning to face another long empty day. Would she try to remember what day it was, so she could take a birth-control pill first? Those are for people with a future. Don't tell me she'd do it as a matter of habit. She wasn't that kind of a girl."

"You think it was an accident?"

"Accidents happen," Shayne said. "But I don't think this was one. She was tired, not drunk. Here's a theory. Listen to the way it sounds. You were there while she was getting ready for bed. The moment she came in, she got herself a glass of water and took a couple of pills. You got rid of the water while she was in the shower. She came out. 'Did I take my pills? I guess not—no water.' Two more. She was finishing up a tense weekend and she couldn't stop thinking about all the interesting things that happened. She went on talking after she was in bed and reached for the bottle. Two more pills. A long goodnight kiss. 'See you in the morning, Ruthie. Don't forget to take your pills.' "

Forbes came to his feet abruptly, then sat down again. Shayne held his eyes for a moment, and swung around on Candida.

"Then you came up. You told her Forbes was in trouble over that old poker debt, and she could help by leaving town for a few days. She agreed—anything to help her boy. You gave her five hundred dollars. There were ten fifties in her purse, separate from the rest of her money, which added up to nine and a half bucks. Then you got her a fresh glass of water so she could take a couple of pills and forget it. Make it three. No, she has to counteract all that benzedrine. Four."

"That's pure fantasy!" Candida snapped. "And you know it."

"I don't know a goddamn thing. All I'm doing is wrapping a couple of guesses around a theory. Maybe you didn't pay Ruth to organize that poker game, but at this point it sure as hell looks like it. A statement from her to that effect would cost United States Chemical two million bucks and put Hal Begley in bankruptcy. You're an ambitious girl, Candida, too ambitious. Success or failure, prestige or exposure—and the whole thing hinged on whether or not Ruth was alive in the morning. When she asked you if you'd seen her taking her sleeping pills, it would be so easy to say no."

"It wouldn't be easy, and it didn't happen."

Shayne laughed unpleasantly. "And what about you, Forbes? Your father has just about had it with you. If I can show that you sold Candida that folder, he'll kick you out of the company and change his will."

"I don't care."

"I don't believe you." The detective lit a cigarette deliberately. "Slavery was abolished years ago. If you don't want the job, quit. You've got a terrible record on your own showing. Add it all up, and a hard-eyed district attorney would get a profile of a spoiled rich kid who wouldn't hesitate a minute about slipping a couple of extra pills to a girl who was that much of a danger to him."

Forbes looked at Shayne defiantly, but there was terror in his eyes.

"Which one of you did it?" Shayne said. "You both had the opportunity. You both have a motive."

Candida looked at Forbes, whose eyes had narrowed. She said warningly, "Don't let him rattle you, Forbes. If it's that bad, we both need a lawyer."

"You won't have time to talk to a lawyer," Shayne said. "Talk to me. I'm not a cop. Nothing's going to be signed here. I can't hurt you with a verbal admission."

"I don't think I'll start trusting you this late in the game."

"I'm setting a deadline—seven tomorrow morning. At five after seven I dump the whole thing in the D.A.'s lap. District attorneys can't leave anything hanging. They have to come up with a solution. If what he comes up with is conspiracy to commit murder, I want you to realize that he can make it stick. The one basic thing to prove is that Forbes was the source of the T-239 folder. Everything follows from that. We can bring in Jake Fitch to testify about the locker-room time sheet. We establish the exact moment the transfer took place, and then we talk to Lou Johnson and find out when he was paid off. If the folder changed hands April twenty-third and Johnson got his money that evening or the next day, what else will a jury need?"

He saw that he had finally managed to reach her. There was a tense line between her eyebrows. Her eyes were steady on his face.

He said less harshly, "How did you make the arrangements, by phone? You couldn't accept anonymous material. You had to have a name to go with it. I've been telling you how this will look to a jury. That doesn't mean I think it happened that way. I think you were fooled, Candida, badly fooled. There's only one person who could do it, and only one way it could be done. One important thing is missing. Until I get that, the rest of it isn't worth a goddamn."

"Stop!" Forbes said. "Tell me one thing. Do you think Ruthie was murdered?"

"Yes," Shayne said bleakly. "And I think it was meant to be written off as a suicide. The fact that you and Candida were with her before she went to sleep couldn't have been arranged in advance. But it gives me a lever, and I mean to use it. You have a choice: talk to me now or the D.A. in the morning."

"I haven't concealed anything," Forbes said sullenly.

Candida picked up her drink. It was a Scotch highball,

nearly full. She tilted the glass higher and higher and set it down empty.

"Forbes sold me the folder," she said.

Forbes shot out of his chair. "How can you lie like that? Whatever Shayne wants to think happened when Ruthie went to bed, I know what happened! She took two sleeping pills and her birth-control pill and asked me to get in with her and hold her until she fell asleep. Then the phone rang. I don't know what you said to her, but it woke her up. She told me to go. If anybody gave her any extra pills, it was you! When I worked on the proofs of the report, I took them home one weekend. Ruthie was with me. Did you hire her to sneak them out to you? Did you?"

He started for Candida. Shayne moved between them.

"Shut up, Forbes! Candida's going to tell us what happened. Sit down and listen."

He backed Forbes into his chair and then returned to Candida.

"O.K., it's the middle of April," he said. "You can see there's no hope of getting what you want out of Walter Langhorne. You're about ready to start putting the heat on Jose Despard. Take it from there."

She held out her glass and he poured Scotch over the ice.

"Hal got a phone call at the office," she said. "It was a man's voice. Hal buzzed me and I listened on an extension. The voice was faint and very fuzzy, as though he was speaking through a tissue stretched over the mouthpiece. Walter had a way of using synonyms for common expressions, and this man did the same thing. But I knew instantly that it wasn't Walter. It was somebody else who wanted us to think it was Walter. He offered us the T-239 material."

"Who suggested the country-club locker?"

"He did. He gave us precise instructions. There were two packages. The first one had every alternate page of the report, pages one, three, five and so on. Hal picked it up. We checked with United States. They were delighted and told us to go ahead. We wrapped thirty thousand dollars in fifties and hundreds and Hal left it in the locker. Somebody picked it up and left the even-numbered pages."

"Somebody!" Forbes said. "We all belong to that club—the company pays for our memberships. What makes you think you can pin it on me?"

Shayne explained,

"The club bartender was one of their people. They gave him a list of Despard executives. He clocked them in and out on the crucial dates."

"And we ruled out everybody but you, Forbes," Candida said. "But we had to be really sure. Walter had told me enough about you and your friends so I knew where to look. I found out about Ruth and your poker losses. I went to New York and tracked down Lou Johnson. I offered to buy your IOU's. He didn't have them. He'd mailed them to a Miami P.O. box. He got his money April twenty-fourth, in fifties and hundreds."

Forbes pushed back his long hair with both hands. *"Is that true?* It can be checked."

"It's true, Forbes."

He looked from Candida to Shayne. "It looks bad, doesn't it? But I didn't do it. I went through a kind of semi-crackup after Mother died. If you have proof I was in the club on the right days, I suppose I was there, but I wasn't playing golf. I didn't call Begley pretending to be Walter. I know nothing at all about this exchange of packages. I didn't give Johnson any money." He threw out both hands. "I'll take a lie-detector test."

Shayne grinned sardonically. "I believe everything you say. That doesn't mean I won't turn you in at seven o'clock tomorrow unless you can give me something more than a simple denial."

"What else can I give you? I've been thinking about it for six months. I haven't been able to move it an inch."

Shayne looked at his watch. "You've got four and a half hours. We won't get anywhere with questions and answers. Whoever rigged this thought of all the questions and made sure of the answers in advance. I wasn't impressed with this soul-session technique when I first heard about it, but I can see it might have possibilities if the people involved really want to make it work. You and

Candida have a pretty good incentive—think up an explanation or go to jail."

He refilled his glass and looked at Candida.

"Forget about T-239 and those locker-room arrangements. All that is incidental. What I want to find out is what you're doing in that crummy job."

"But what possible connection—"

He rode her down. "You're sleeping with Begley, aren't you? Do you have any respect for him, in bed or any other place? It took me ten seconds to see that you have the makings of a very nice girl. What happened to you?"

She had fallen back, her eyes burning in her dead-white face. He continued to hold her eyes. "You recognized the real thing when you met Walter Langhorne, in spite of the fact that he was twice your age. You couldn't bring yourself to set him up for the usual blackmail squeeze. That left you with Jose. Think about those infrared photographs for a minute. You didn't want to go ahead with that mess, did you? You're not as tough as you think. You jumped at the telephone offer without insisting on a face-to-face meeting, which is against all the rules. Even so, how do you think that kid Deedee is going to turn out? She's seventeen. Her parents threw her out of the house.—I think I'll get her in on this," he added suddenly. "It might do her some good."

"Don't," Candida said faintly.

Shayne wheeled on Forbes. "What attracted you to Ruth Di Palma? Forget about the jams you've been in over the years. Just stay with that one point. I only saw her for ten minutes, but I liked her. But she wasn't for you, and she had the sense to know it. What hooked you?"

There was a thoughtful expression on the boy's handsome dark face. He poured some whiskey. Candida moved to the terrace. After waiting a moment, Shayne made several quiet-voiced phone calls.

When Candida came back, she sat on the foot of the bed facing Forbes's chair.

"I think he's right. I don't want to talk about the points he raised about me. Not right now. Later I think I can. I'm wondering about the stories you write. They meant something special to Walter. Do you think you're really a writer, or is it just something to keep from thinking of yourself as a rich boy with a rich father?"

Shayne checked the level in the cognac bottle and put it on the floor. He sat down with his back against the wall, lit a cigarette and settled down to listen.

CHAPTER 18

When Jose Despard arrived, looking gray and distraught, Shayne took him to the terrace and explained the ground rules. If they found the answer he wanted by seven in the morning, it was possible that Jose's adventure with Deedee would never become public knowledge.

"Those pictures you mentioned," Despard said in his worried voice. "I hope you'll give me first refusal. If you'd be willing to take a monthly installment, I could work something out."

"If I have to make a case against Forbes and Candida, everything goes in, the pictures included. So cooperate."

"Oh, dear. Well, I'll do what I can."

Deedee showed up fifteen minutes later. Her arrival created a stir. Despard spilled his drink. Candida blushed slightly. Deedee said a general hello and headed for the bottles. Shayne gave her a Coke.

"*That* kind of party," she said in disgust.

When Jake Fitch came in soon afterward, no one noticed. Forbes and his uncle were shouting bitterly at each other.

Shayne's only contribution was to ration the liquor and see that the disputes stopped short of blows. Time passed. The group broke down into smaller groups and came back together. Between five and six everyone seemed to sag at the same time, and Shayne thought it might be over. Then Jose, brooding in silence on one of the beds, broke out with an accusation that Forbes had never really loved his mother, in spite of having been the most important single thing in her life.

"Did I ask to be?" Forbes demanded. "It was too much! We're telling the truth now, Jose. I was embarrassed to be with her."

"Embarrassed! By Cicely? She always had beautiful manners."

"But she was a bit of a hypocrite, wasn't she?"

An hour later Shayne remembered his seven-o'clock deadline. Without telling anyone of the change, he set a new deadline two hours later. When he next looked at his watch, it was five after nine. He carried the phone into the bathroom and shut the door on the cord.

First he called Tim Rourke at the *News,* to ask if he had access to a portable microfilm viewer. Rourke thought he could locate one, and meanwhile he wanted to know what had happened. Shayne told him he could find out by coming to room 1229 of the Hotel St. Albans.

After that, he called the Despard office and asked if the company president had returned from Washington. The plane, he was told, would arrive at the Opa-Locka Airport within the next half hour. Shayne phoned the airport and left an urgent message to be handed to Hallam as he stepped off the plane. Then he began calling Beach hotels.

Fletcher Perkins, president of United States Chemical, was registered at the Deauville but he didn't answer his phone. Shayne had him paged, and pulled him out of the coffee shop where he was having breakfast.

"This is Michael Shayne," he said wearily, "and I hope we can skip the preliminaries. Hal Begley was telling you about me last night."

"Yes."

"He may have passed on a proposition I made to him—an even trade of a three-month postponement for an agreement to drop all legal action. That was window-dressing, Mr. Perkins, and I hope you haven't wasted any time thinking about it."

"I didn't let it keep me awake. I don't think I quite know what you mean by the expression 'window-dressing.' "

His crisp voice made Shayne realize all at once just how groggy he himself was. He made an effort to collect his thoughts.

"I've been fired by Despard's, and I had no authority to make an offer. I've been operating since then for my own account. I have a new proposition, and this is the real one. It'll cost you eight thousand, the balance of the fee I was going to get from Hallam. You were told that Forbes, Jr., supplied the paint folder. He didn't. He had nothing to do with it, and I'm about to break the news to a few people. If you can come to room twelve twenty-nine at the St. Albans, I won't have to repeat myself."

"And why would this be worth eight thousand dollars? I know your reputation. Possibly you don't know mine. I've never yet bought a pig in a poke."

"This particular pig is worth more than eight thousand," Shayne told him. "But I've been up all night and I'm too tired to haggle. Come over and listen. I'm not asking you for payment in advance."

"I just may do that, Shayne," Perkins said thoughtfully. "It seemed to me that Begley looked a little white around the gills. I'm curious to find out why. I'll be there in ten minutes."

Shayne went to sleep with the phone in his lap, waking when someone opened the bathroom door. He returned to the other room as Tim Rourke arrived, weighed down by a heavy piece of equipment. He set it on a bureau and looked around the room with unconcealed astonishment.

"Mike, what have you got cooking here?"

Shayne followed his look, seeing the room and its occupants as they would seem to a newcomer. The men were haggard, unshaven, very much on edge. Deedee was still wearing the dress Shayne had put her into twelve hours before, and that was all she was wearing. Having been more untidy than Candida to begin with, the night had changed her less. Candida had stopped thinking about how she looked hours earlier. Her careful makeup had worn away. Her sweater was partially unbuttoned. She was sitting on a bed, her legs up. Forbes, in a chair beside her, was down to his T-shirt. In spite of the stale air, in spite of everyone's obvious pallor and fatigue, there was an unmistakable feeling of suppressed excitement in the room.

"We've just been killing time," Shayne told his friend. "The boy has the key to this, but he doesn't know it. He has to find it himself. Two more people are going to be joining us. Let them in and tell them not to interrupt."

He returned to his place beside the cognac bottle. Deedee leaned across him.

"This is a real neat party, Mr. Shayne. I'm going to give one for the gang at school. You aren't still sore at me, are you, about that whip?"

He moved her out of the way. "I want to hear this."

Forbes was saying angrily, "I know how old Ruthie was. Five years older than I am. Five years—that doesn't make her a mother."

Shayne put in, "And she wasn't anything like your mother either, was she?"

"Not a damn bit. She didn't look like her, she didn't behave like her. There was no resemblance at all."

Jose said, "Cicely did look something like her when she was the same age."

"And what's that supposed to imply?" Forbes demanded hotly. "When I went to bed with her I was committing incest?"

"No," Jose said doubtfully. "Don't be so touchy."

Shayne leaned forward, his arm around Deedee's shoulder so she wouldn't swing and block his view. "You were embarrassed when you were with your mother. Why?"

"I don't know. It wasn't—" He held up for an instant, then plunged on. "It was when we were all together, Mother and Dad. There was this strain. With Dad, there's always so much *effort* involved in everything he does. Being a father is like a role. He plays the stern father. I play the unruly son. We both know there's nothing to it. It's not real."

"You don't think he's really your father?"

"That's not what I mean. It's—"

He stopped short, staring at Shayne. Everyone was watching him.

"God, I wonder," he said slowly.

Jose objected, "Cicely was hardly the type to indulge in illicit relations outside her marriage."

"Shut up!" Candida snapped. "What do you know about anybody?"

"She was my sister, damn it! There may not have been any passionate love in that marriage, but she knew the meaning of the word 'duty.' "

"Obviously," Candida said sarcastically. "From what Walter told me, bringing Hallam into the family was the thing that saved the Despard fortunes. Without him you would have foundered years ago."

There was a light double knock at the door. Shayne heard it, and so did Tim Rourke, but the others were too preoccupied. Rourke opened the door to admit a stranger, a small neat man with black-rimmed glasses and gray hair parted in the middle. Rourke whispered something to him. He shrugged.

Candida was telling Forbes, "That's why it was so hard for you to live up to your father's requirements. That's why you thought Ruthie and her bunch were so wonderful. You couldn't invent a group more exactly the opposite of Forbes Hallam, Senior."

"One time I was home from school on vacation," Forbes said carefully. "I found her diary in the attic. I didn't know it was a diary or I wouldn't have read it. It looked like a plain notebook. After I got started I couldn't stop. It gave such a picture of the way she lived just after she was married. Then all at once there was a change of tone. She did the same things, but now she was enthusiastic about them. There'd be an entry about a boat ride or a strawberry party with a group of friends. And then on a separate line, on a line by itself, there'd be an exclamation point. Or two. Once, after an entry about a picnic on an island, there were three. I haven't thought about it for years. It was before I was born. I never did figure out those exclamation points."

"You didn't let yourself figure them out," Shayne said. "Because if you'd counted nine months from one of those exclamation points, you must have known it would bring you down to the day you were born."

There was silence.

Rourke opened the door again. This time, when Forbes Hallam, Sr., came in, carrying a small suitcase, the tension broke. Hallam looked as tired as everybody else, but in a different way.

He said abruptly, "What's the meaning of this?" After looking around the room, he snapped, "Put on your shirt, Forbes!"

"Does it matter?" Forbes asked wearily.

Shayne stood up and stretched. "The night's over. Do what your father says, Forbes. Get dressed. Anybody who wants another drink get it now. The bar's about to close."

"Perkins!" Hallam exclaimed, seeing the president of Despard's chief competitor. "What are you doing here?"

The other shrugged. "Don't ask me. Ask Shayne."

Shayne grinned. "He's trying to make up his mind whether anything I have to say could possibly be worth eight thousand bucks. We haven't said a word about T-239 since one-thirty this morning, but now we're about to get back to the dull subject of paint. Have you realized yet, Mr. Perkins, that your company's been swindled?"

The word dropped like a stone. The Boston industrialist looked at Candida, his face suddenly nasty.

Shayne plugged in the tabletop microfilm viewer. Taking out the little reel of film he had found in the locked box in Candida's bedroom, he fitted it into place. A strip of reinforced tape kept the film from slipping. Shayne used the scalpel to cut it loose. Rourke helped him thread the loose end into the empty sprocket. He snapped on the light inside the machine and turned the crank.

"There's no doubt in anybody's mind that T-239 is a wonderful paint," he said. "But Forbes said something that's been picking at me for two days. He said there was an earlier version of the paint. It licked the peeling problem, but after a certain amount of exposure to the weather, white paint turned yellow. Probably the formula wasn't much different from the one they finally used."

He found the page he wanted. "Despard, you're the R. and D. man. You remember what went into the first batch. Take a look at this."

Despard put on his glasses. Bending over the viewer, he peered into its lighted interior and sharpened the focus. His lips moved as he read to himself.

Suddenly he broke into his high, nervous giggle and looked at Hallam.

"You dog, you," he said roguishly.

CHAPTER 19

Hallam's expression remained unchanged, but Perkins took a backward step, looking as though he had taken a hard punch in the stomach. His tanned face had gone yellow, like the first batches of T-239.

"I want to use the phone."

"When I'm finished," Shayne told him. "And don't look at Candida. She's a fellow victim. She was tricked into passing on a copy of the report that was completely authentic in every respect except one. The recipe in it was for the original mixture, before it was modified as a result of performance records in the early tests. Does everybody understand what I'm saying? To put it another way, the performance figures were genuine, but they applied to the final version, after various things were switched around or modified. Planting fake information is an old spy technique. It happens all the time in the cold war. The paint United States Chemical is announcing on television tomorrow morning will look fine in the cans, but it'll turn yellow before the end of the first season. And as soon as the bad news begins to come in, United States will be up for grabs. After a coup like this, Hallam's own position in his firm will be impregnable."

"I have to hand it to you," Jose told his brother-in-law.

"Nobody like you Yankees to see tricky ways to make a dollar."

"Don't congratulate him yet," Shayne said. "His problem now is that his idea was a little too good."

Hallam, still stony-faced, picked up an unclaimed glass of whiskey and drained it, watched by a half dozen pairs of eyes.

"First time I ever saw you take a drink at nine-thirty in the morning," Despard observed.

"I didn't sleep last night," Hallam said defensively. "Now this—this nonsense."

"How can you say it's nonsense?" Jose said. "You've done some tricky things in your time, but this takes the blue ribbon. Don't get me wrong. I'm all for it. It's great, fantastic. It's just not something I could have come up with myself. I don't have that kind of mentality."

"You fool." Hallam gave him a baleful look. "Just because this wild man makes an unprovable assertion—"

"You're the only one who could have done it," Shayne said roughly. "That's been obvious all along. Jake."

The bartender looked up vaguely. "Want me?"

"When you were keeping that time sheet on the Despard executives last April, was this man in the club on either of the important days?"

Jake's eyes swung to Hallam, who returned his look stolidly. "Mr. Hallam Senior? His name wasn't even on the list."

"I know that. Nobody suspected the president of the company of selling company secrets."

"Well," Jake said slowly, rubbing his chin, "I wouldn't be too surprised if he was in. I didn't see him so much lately, but when I first went to work there he was in and out all the time."

"All right, Jake," Shayne said. "You can go home now."

"No, thanks, Mike, I'm having a good time just sitting here."

Shayne went on, "Hallam had to be sure his son was in the club the day he planted the report, and again the day he picked up the money. That wouldn't be too hard to arrange. The reason he's drinking whiskey so soon after breakfast is that he tried to do two things at once, outmaneuver a business rival and disinherit an illegitimate son." His voice hardened. "Sit down, Hallam."

"That won't be necessary. I'm not staying."

"How long have you known that Forbes isn't your son?"

Hallam took a step toward the door, trying to leave. The whiskey had hit him hard. He stayed to hear Shayne supply his own answer.

"A year at least. Candida's no dumbbell. You couldn't just send her the report anonymously through the mail. She had to be convinced that she was dealing with somebody who needed money and didn't care where it came from. This part of the plan began to move when Forbes told you he needed money because his girl was pregnant. You said you'd take care of it, as you'd taken care of so many other emergencies for him. There's one book in Ruth's room—the only book. It's called *Thirty Easy Steps to a Richer, Fuller Life,* and she read it so many times it's falling apart. She was a setup for a father who claimed to be at his wits' end about what to do with his irresponsible son. Somehow Forbes had to be made to realize that this is a cold world. He needed a taste of real trouble. How about this? What if he lost some money to a professional gambler, and his father refused to help? Nothing too serious would happen. He'd have to sell his car and pay off the debt in monthly chunks, and maybe he'd finally settle down to work. Ruth agreed to set up a poker game." He turned to Forbes. "How does it sound so far?"

Forbes was chewing on a knuckle. "Go on."

Perkins put in, "I'll promise you one thing, Candida Morse. I'll put you and Hal Begley out of business if it's the last thing I do."

She raised her glass to him. "Hal doesn't know it yet, but I've resigned."

"Everything went according to schedule," Shayne continued. "You probably thought everything would be out in the open by now, didn't you, Hallam? It must have seemed to you that Forbes would stick out like a sore thumb, as the only real possibility. The trouble was, both Jose and

Langhorne were also under suspicion, and Forbes himself was conducting the investigation. That's why you brought me in. You were afraid Perkins might get cold feet at the last minute. If Forbes, Junior, your only son, was fired and cut out of your will for stealing that folder, it would remove any lingering doubts in Perkins's mind that the material was genuine. Everything in this case has been the opposite of the way it seemed. You ordered me off last night, not because you really wanted me off, but because you knew that was the surest way of pointing me at Forbes and keeping me going."

Forbes's face was working. "Dad—"

His father refused to look at him.

"It's a question of principle," Shayne explained. "He's worked too hard all his life. When his wife was in the hospital, he stumbled across her diary. It must have been a bad shock. He didn't want everything he'd worked so hard for to go to somebody else's son. But it wasn't simple. Because of his shaky position in the company, he couldn't just change his will without explanation, without the approval of the rest of the family. He couldn't get that for a small matter like a pregnancy or losing too much money at poker. Those are typical Despard jams. But betraying the company, betraying the family's financial interests—you wouldn't stand for that, would you, Jose?"

"Absolutely not. If any son of mine did a thing like that, I'd disinherit the bastard myself." He giggled. "Don't take the word literally, Forbes."

Hallam managed to speak at last. "I don't apologize for turning Forbes down when he asked for money to buy back those IOU's. I should have drawn that line years ago. Why not talk to the Di Palma girl? She'll tell you how little truth there is in your trumped-up story."

"She's dead," Shayne said bleakly. "She died at one-thirty this morning."

Hallam reached for more whiskey. Shayne poured it for him and let him drink in silence.

"And she's not our only death," Shayne said. "We don't want to forget Walter Langhorne."

"You were there. You know it was an accident."

Shayne shook his head and said wearily, "Nothing you've done has been accidental. When Forbes read his mother's diary, all he saw was a set of exclamation points. You saw something else. You're the kind of man who keeps careful records. I think you checked the dates on those excursions your wife took the year before Forbes was born, and I think you came up with a name."

Jose protested, "Shayne, if what you're trying to say is that my sister committed adultery with Walter Langhorne" —he checked himself and finished more tentatively— "you're wrong. You're dead wrong."

Shayne went on speaking directly to Hallam. "That shooting-blind setup was too good not to use. Langhorne had been talking about leaving the company, and you might not get another chance. So you shot him. There was never any question about that. The only thing missing was a motive. Why would somebody murder an old friend and frame his own son? Put the two things together and the answer is obvious."

"You're lying!" Hallam spat out.

"You know I'm not lying. You told him why you had to shoot him. When he couldn't argue you out of it, he tried to grab your gun. You shot from the hip as he came at you, and honor was satisfied. There may even be people who'll think you did the only possible thing you could do. But nobody's going to like hearing what happened to Ruth. You'll go to the gas chamber for that, Hallam. You probably took the precaution of burning the diary. Ruth was the only person left who could tie you to any of this."

Hallam wet his lips. "I was in Washington last night. How could I have anything to do with—"

Shayne broke in. "And I've been wondering why you went all the way to Washington for a legal conference which you could have handled just as well by phone. Especially since somebody told me you don't pay much attention to lawyers' advice."

He pulled out Ruth's circular pillbox. "Do you know what this is?"

Hallam's eyes flicked down to the box, then back to the detective's face. "Some kind of medication? Get to the point. I have people waiting at the office."

"I have a feeling they're going to be waiting a long time."

He took a step toward Hallam. The smaller man stood his ground for only a moment before falling back toward the terrace.

"If you hit me, Shayne," he warned, "I'll make you wish you hadn't."

"When Ruth died you were a thousand miles away, and I'm sure you arranged to be seen, at intervals on and off all night. These are birth-control pills, for the benefit of those who may not know. Hallam knows. Each one is dated. Last night's pill is missing. You've been seeing her right along, haven't you? Carefully, very very carefully, the way you do everything."

"No."

"You've been giving her money. Yesterday was the tenth day of her new cycle. You saw her sometime during the last ten days and switched pillboxes. It's a standard drug-store item. Both boxes were precisely the same, except that in the new box the tenth pill wasn't the usual hormone preparation. It looked the same, but it actually contained a lethal dose of barbiturates."

Hallam, his eyes held by Shayne's, was breathing shallowly. The room was quiet until Despard said coldly, "Talk about sneaks."

Hallam made an effort. "You can't be serious. How could anybody—"

"An ordinary person probably couldn't," Shayne said. "For the head of a chemical company it wouldn't be hard. So Ruth took the pill, along with a few of her regular sleeping pills, and died. All the autopsy will show is an overdose of barbiturates."

"Brilliant!" Jose exclaimed. "Not the kind of thing I could do myself, but it shows a certain warped intelligence."

Shayne waited, his eyes on Hallam's. Now he would see if the long night's preparation had paid off. Hallam had to be forced to justify himself. The atmosphere was beginning to affect him. This was a room where a half dozen people had spent the night speaking the truth.

His jaw muscles flickered.

Jose gave his idiotic half giggle. "His wife betrays him and he shoots the man. Naturally. But twenty-five years later! And a birth-control pill. Jesus God. Hallam, everybody always knew you were nothing but a twerp."

Veins stood out on Hallam's forehead. The unexpected mildness of Jose's condemnation had an odd result. Some of his tension left him. His eyes had closed, but now he opened them and looked at Shayne mildly.

Jose said, "I always did like murder trials. I surely expect to enjoy this one because I'm going to be in it. I never would have thought of it without your inspiration, Shayne —you're a wizard, man, I mean it—but I stayed late one night to catch up on my correspondence—no, to tell you the truth I had a date later—and I saw him."

"Hallam?" Shayne said quietly.

"Who else? In the laboratory. With the pill mold."

Hallam broke his connection with Shayne with a twitch. He looked at his son. His lips parted in a terrible drawn smile.

"Well, I'm sorry he stayed late. I'm sorry about Ruthie. She was better than everybody. If you want to be a literary man, Forbes, go ahead and be one. If you hate businessmen, you have no right to live off dividends. Do you understand? I didn't change my will. Too many things to do. Offer Perkins eight million for his company. No more than eight. He has to accept. Don't let the Despards—"

He whirled and broke for the terrace, moving fast. Shayne, who was nearest, reacted slowly. He collided with Perkins in the doorway, and Hallam was over the railing by the time the detective reached it.

Shayne swiped at him awkwardly with his hook, but missed. Hallam fell away, face up, arms and legs splayed outward, an expression of astonishment on his face. A girl screamed in the room.

Shayne turned without waiting to see Hallam hit the

concrete twelve floors below. Jose, rubbing his mouth, was watching him.

Shayne said, "Did you really see him in the lab?"

Jose snorted. "Don't get high and mighty with me, Shayne. You know as well as I do you couldn't get a conviction. You were a little slow there, I thought. I've seen you move, man. You move like a rattlesnake—when you want to."

After a moment Shayne said heavily. "It's been a hard night. Now it's time for the cops."

THE SECRET OF SANTA VITTORIA

by Robert Crichton

THE NATION'S #1 BESTSELLER

From time immemorial the Italian hill town of Santa Vittoria had existed as a world unto itself, hostile to strangers, wholly involved in growing and making the fat black wine that was its glory and its lifeblood. As the Allied armies approached, the Germans sent an occupying force to claim the town's great treasure—one million bottles of wine. At this moment a leader emerged—the clownish wine merchant Bombolini. Behind him the town united, forgetting ancient feuds, lovers' rivalries, the division between aristocrat and peasant, pooling its energies and resources to outwit the invader.

"This brilliant novel should be celebrated with a fanfare of trumpets, with festivals in the streets." —*The New York Times*

"Crichton tells his story with grace, pace, warmth, and a wonderful free-reeling wit that skips among the vineyards like an inebriated billygoat." —*Time Magazine*

95¢